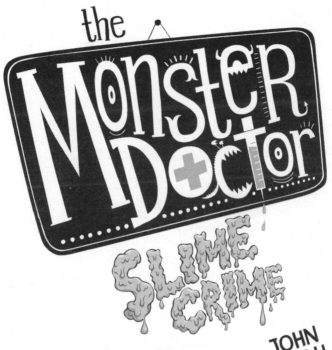

the MONSTER DOCTOR

SLIME CRIME

JOHN KELLY

Books by John Kelly

Monster Doctor
Monster Doctor: Revolting Rescue
Monster Doctor: Slime Crime

And Coming Soon

Monster Doctor: Foul Play

First published 2021 by Macmillan Children's Books
an imprint of Pan Macmillan
The Smithson, 6 Briset Street, London EC1M 5NR
EU representative: Macmillan Publishers Ireland Limited,
Mallard Lodge, Lansdowne Village, Dublin 4
Associated companies throughout the world
www.panmacmillan.com

ISBN 978-1-5290-2131-8

1 3 5 7 9 8 6 4 2

A CIP catalogue record for this book is available
from the British Library.

Printed and bound by CPI Group (UK) Ltd, Croydon CR0 4YY

MIX
Paper from
responsible sources
FSC® C016486

Dear reader,
I wrote this especially for you.

CONTENTS:

Look out for words with the doctor's symbol
after them and look them up in the glossary.

'IS IT A LEAFY GREEN?'

Chapter 1

The monster doctor's voice crackled from the heavy **walkie-talkie** radio dangling on my belt. *'What is the exact colour of the boil, Nurse Ozzy? Over!'*

I didn't reply because at that precise moment both of my hands were terribly busy preventing me from falling off the top of a hundred-foot-tall ladder. To distract myself from the **dreadful drop** below, I examined the huge boil that was six inches from my face. It was roughly the size of an over-inflated **space hopper** and looked very angry indeed.

The boil was attached to the end of an enormous nose, and that nose was attached to an equally enormous giant called Little Lionel. (Lionel is small for a giant. Hence his name. Most **giants** are about two-hundred-feet tall, so at almost half that height Lionel is probably borderline ogre, to be honest.)

'Come in, Nurse Ozzy!' said the doctor's insistent voice. *'I repeat: what colour is—'*

'I CAN'T REACH THE RADIO!' I bellowed down towards where the doctor stood holding the bottom of the wobbly ladder. The animated **blob** of messy hair, tweed and industrial-framed glasses that is Annie von Sichertall – a.k.a. the monster doctor, a.k.a. my boss – looked up at me. And, not for the first time, I wondered why it was me perched dangerously on top of this ladder examining **a giant's boil,** instead of the monster doctor herself.

When we arrived, we had extended the roof ladder from Lance, the ambulance.

I'd assumed (wrongly, of course) that the doctor would climb it. After all, it was her turn.

Instead, she just stood there, looking at me expectantly.

'No!' I'd said firmly. 'I did the last suicidally dangerous thing. It's your turn!'

The doctor had responded with a very convincing reason as to why she couldn't climb up. Well, it had seemed very **convincing** at the time, but now I couldn't remember what it was. It was something about her **dodgy left knee,** or an insurance policy having lapsed. I forget which.

'Nurse Ozzy!' her voice gently chided me from the radio. *'A monster doctor never shouts in front of a patient – unless they insist on lecturing you about a silly treatment they've found on the monsterweb. Then you can really let rip at—'*

'THE BOIL IS BRIGHT GREEN!' I shouted in order to cut off her rambling.

'Ah! Now that's rather interesting,' she said. *'Would you say it was a leafy green? Or closer to the lovely bright green of freshly exuded troll pus?'*

I thought about that for a moment. After three weeks as the monster doctor's assistant, I was now well acquainted with all the wondrous shades of troll pus.

'NEITHER,' I shouted down. 'IT'S MORE LIKE THE CHUNKY BITS IN DELORES'S *PISTACHIO* AND *PHLEGM* BISCUITS.' Delores is our surgery's grumpy receptionist. I can't decide which is more scary: Delores or the contents of her special biscuit tin.

Somewhere around my ankles I felt Lionel's mouth begin to open. Oh no! He was going to speak again. I grabbed on tightly to the ladder.

'SPOT...NOT...THERE...AT... BREAKFAST!' he said in a voice as slow and as loud as a passing car stereo.

Giants aren't stupid, by the way. The reason they speak like that is because their **brains** are so MASSIVE that it can take a while for information to travel from point A to point B. (Like when you're trying to show your mum and dad how a new TV works.)

'EXTRAORDINARY!' exclaimed the doctor. **'So this boil is almost as fast-growing as a human teenager's acne!'** She went silent for a moment.

This was worrying. When the monster doctor goes quiet, it usually means one of three things:

1. She has run away.
2. She is stuck in the pharmacy cupboard again. (We should really get that door fixed.)
3. She's about to ask me to do something very **dangerous** and is thinking of a nice way to put it.

'Ozzy,' she continued in a suspiciously innocent voice, **'I wonder if you might just give the boil a gentle tap and measure how much it wobbles.'**

'I'VE ALREADY DONE THAT,' I shouted smugly. I happened to have read about Diagnostic **Jellification** the previous night in my wonderful *Monster Maladies* book. It contains tons of information about the most common monster illnesses out there and it has a lot of really useful stuff that **every trainee monster doctor** needs to know – it is especially helpful for trainees who are human, like me. For instance, there's a very useful section at the beginning about running very fast.

Diagnostic Jellification

Diagnostic Jellification is how monster doctors are able to measure exactly how **rubbery** a patient – or part of a patient – is. This can be an extremely useful thing for a medical professional to know. Especially if they are about to try to stick something **sharp** into the patient, like a **needle**. Some monsters' skin is so soft that it can be pierced with a **breadstick**, while others may require the use of a rocket-propelled armour-piercing syringe.

The DJ scale begins with extremely **sloppy** and **gloopy** substances like fresh dog drool (0.0 DJs), custard (1.8 DJs) and jellified creatures like blobs (3.5ish DJs).

At the opposite end of the scale you will find much harder materials like steel (8.8 DJs), **Collososaur armour-plating** (9.6 DJs) and even dried-on breakfast cereal (10.0 DJs).

'IT'S NOT VERY WOBBLY!' I shouted. 'I'D RATE IT AT ABOUT 4.5 DJs.' (Well-inflated space hopper.)

'That's not right,' mused the doctor. 'A boil that size should have a squishy consistency somewhere between Bob the Blob and human brains or blancmange. You'd better take a sample, Nurse Ozzy. There's a medium monster needle in your kit.'

I shifted very carefully on the rickety ladder and rooted around in the emergency medical kit dangling from my right shoulder. My fingers closed on a needle that would have made a pretty useful **spear point for a Spartan warrior.**

'I'm very sorry,' I said, holding the huge syringe up in front of Lionel's giant crossed eyes. 'But I need to use this.'

9

Fortunately, monsters aren't as *squeamish* about needles as humans are.

'NO . . . PROBLEM . . .' he boomed. 'ONLY . . . A . . . TEENY . . . WEENY . . . LITTLE . . . NEEDLE.'

He laughed gently, almost knocking me off the ladder. But I held on grimly until the ladder – and my teeth – stopped rattling.

'Remember, Ozzy!' the doctor's voice fuzzed once again through the radio. *'Giants are as thick-skinned as reality TV talent show candidates. You'll have to give it a bit of welly.'*

So I gripped the syringe, took a deep breath and imagined that I was trying to cut a piece of my gran's pastry.

I swung the needle down with as much force as I could and, as the sharp point **PUNCTURED** the tough skin of the boil, there was a noise that reminded me of mealtimes at home.

It was a louder version of the noise my baby sister makes when she suddenly decides that the food she has been *chewing* would be better back on the plate. Or on the nearby wall. Or my face.

It was a

SPLAT!

But much, much, **louder.**

And all of a sudden I was very wet and the same colour as the chunky bits in one of Delores's biscuits.

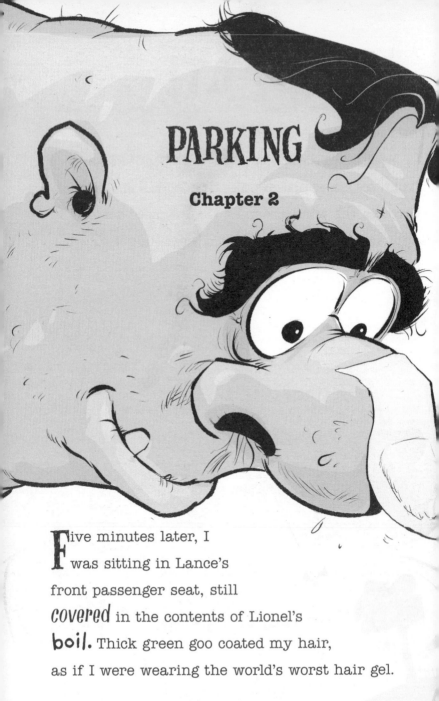

PARKING

Chapter 2

Five minutes later, I was sitting in Lance's front passenger seat, still **covered** in the contents of Lionel's **boil.** Thick green goo coated my hair, as if I were wearing the world's worst hair gel.

And my sweatshirt was so **contaminated** that it would probably have to be burned, then the ashes disposed of somewhere in the middle of the Atlantic Ocean.

I sat scooping handfuls of the **ghastly goo** from my jeans pockets and watched *grumpily* through the windscreen as the monster doctor applied a plaster the size of a small duvet to Lionel's nose.

She waved goodbye to the giant and jumped into Lance's* driving seat.

The monster doctor smiled broadly and clapped me on the shoulder.

'**A boil exploding** in the face is so refreshing, isn't it?' she said. I obviously didn't look refreshed because she added, 'Of course! How thoughtless of me. I always forget that you ordinaries have this **weird aversion to bodily fluids**. Never mind. You can have a nice shower when we get back to the surgery, now that the leak in the *swamp-spa treatment room* has finally been mended.'

She switched on Bruce, the BAT-NAV. This involved **whacking** the side of his jar to wake him up.

16

* Bruce is a monster bat. Monster bats can find their way around the six dimensions of inter-dimensional space with their eyes closed. Although exactly why they do this is a mystery, since they can see perfectly well. Anyway, it is incredibly clever and useful. Which is why every Inter-dimensional Vehicle (IDV), like Lance, comes with a free BAT-NAV to help them navigate.

Bruce's* screen lit up.

> ## OH, IT'S YOU.
> ## I WAS HAVING A LOVELY DREAM
> ## ABOUT A DARK DANK CAVE –

His eyes suddenly alighted on me and he gave an evil little smile.

> ## OOOH! I LIKE OZZY'S NEW HAIRSTYLE!

Did I mention that Bruce is very *rude* to everyone?

But he likes to be especially rude to me.

'Now, Bruce,' chided the doctor. 'Do please try and be *nice* to Ozzy. He's had a difficult morning. And be so kind as to take us back to the surgery via a nice quiet route this time. I do NOT want to travel through the **"very hairy"** dimension today, please.'

> # YOU'RE SO BORING.
> # WE NEVER GET TO DO ANYTHING DANGEROUS
> # SINCE YOU HIRED THE HUMAN.

But he did as he was told and we were immediately transported into inter-dimensional space.*

* We human beings (or 'ordinaries' as monsters know us) live in dimension 3.14, but there are actually six main dimensions. Each one contains lots of sub-dimensions where countless monsters, creatures and things live. It helps to think of inter-dimensional space as a rainbow spectrum of different realities. Realities just like our own but much, much weirder, with more teeth and tentacles.

Thankfully, this time, we had a nice quiet trip home.

The bottom of the Pacific Ocean was peaceful (as rush hour had just finished) and aisle fourteen (barbecues and lawn furniture) at the North Pole branch of B&Q was as *deserted* as usual.

Finally, we emerged on to Lovecraft Avenue and trundled down the road towards the surgery.

As we drew closer, Lance began to rev his engine **aggressively.** Which was very odd, as Lance is usually such a gentle monster.

The doctor patted his steering wheel. **'Steady on, Lance,'** she soothed. 'Calm down, boy! I'm sure it's not a deliberate insult. Yes, I know it's very clearly marked as your bay.'

'What's the matter?' I asked.

Bruce's screen pinged.

ISN'T IT OBVIOUS? SOME IDIOT HAS PARKED IN LANCE'S SPOT!

The doctor pointed to where a large, shiny black car was parked in Lance's **EMERGENCY WAITING BAY.**

Its bonnet was turned up, in what somehow looked like a rather smug, self-satisfied air. And I could have **SWORN** there was a sneer on the overly shiny bumper.

'Lance gets upset if someone parks in his spot?' I laughed.

NO PARKING!

BY ORDER OF LANCE

But that was a *mistake*. Lance growled angrily at me, like my dog Piglet does when I touch his squeaky squirrel without permission.

'Ozzy!' hissed the doctor. 'PLEASE be careful what you say about parking! YOU might not think it's a big deal, but Lance is an Inter-dimensional Vehicle and they have very – very – **strict rules about parking.'**

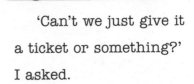

'Can't we just give it a ticket or something?' I asked.

'Oh, dear me, no!' said the doctor. 'It's much too serious an **offence** for that. As you know, IDVs can travel anywhere in any dimension at will, but, sadly, as you also know, **the poor things have a dreadful sense of direction.** Just try and imagine what it feels like to take decades getting back home from the shops, only to discover that another IDV has nicked your precious parking spot!

I can assure you, Ozzy, wars have been fought over less!'

I supposed that did explain an awful lot about the **tense conversations** my dad sometimes has with **Mr Woffell** at number 37.

'Anyway, I can't trust Lance to park himself now,' added the doctor. 'He might "accidentally on purpose" smash that car into tiny pieces. And then smash those pieces into even smaller ones. And then drive back and forth over them a few times. **Be a dear and pop inside and tell the idiot owner to move it?'**

I ran into the surgery as the doctor chaperoned a growling Lance off towards the garage. Despite her best efforts, Lance still managed to 'accidentally on purpose' swipe off the other car's shiny wing mirror. He disappeared round the corner, his engine revving in a happy little laugh.

The surgery was packed with patients. Simon Salamander, the owner of **The Battered Squid chippy,** was there with his front legs covered in dozens of sticky plasters. (He'd obviously been wrestling with the lunchtime specials again.)

My old zombie pal Morty Mort called out, 'Wotcha, Ozzy!' and waved with his right arm. This arm, his torso and his left leg were poking out from a **BRAINSBURY'S carrier bag,** while his head, left arm, feet and nose were distributed between two other *MESSCO carrier bags.*

He'd clearly gone to pieces again – and there was no sign of his right leg anywhere.

'That'll teach me to enrol in mixed **martial arts** classes!' he said, laughing. In fact, he laughed so hard his head rolled off the chair.

Vlad the vampire, who was sitting next to him, leaned forward. He caught Morty's head neatly and popped it safely back on the chair.

'Morty, my very good friend,' he said seriously in his thick **Transylvanian accent,** 'you muzt learn to treat being dead viz more respect!'

Vlad ran the all-night garage and convenience store down the road, and we were treating him for a very nasty case of sunburn. **His wife, Vladness, elbowed him in the ribs and laughed.**

'Muzt you always be zo gloomy, Vlad?' she said. 'Let Morty live a little! After all, ze poor fellow will only be dead vonce!'

I coughed loudly and said, 'Excuse me, everyone!' But the various monsters, things and assorted **un-classified creatures** were all too busy chatting to notice me. So I picked up the *bell-bug* the doctor uses to signal the surgery is open and rang it. *It CLANGED loudly* and they all turned to look. 'Does anyone here drive a shiny black IDV with the number plate I1YR CA5H?'

Nobody answered me. I looked around with a frown, and noticed that there was a monster I didn't recognize talking to Delores the receptionist. The monster looked an awful lot like a **T. Rex** – apart from the fact that it was wearing high heels and a very expensive pinstripe business suit, and was no larger than a well-fed Great Dane. (The dog, obviously. Not the nationality.)

'Excuse me,' I said. 'Is that your car outsi—?'

Delores held up a single tentacle in that annoying **talk-to-the-tentacle-thing** she does when she's extremely 'busy'. She normally does this when she's reading a magazine, painting her tentacle tips or eating a chocolate-covered beetle.

'As I was saying,' she continued, turning back to the miniature dinosaur, 'before I was so RUDELY interrupted –' she scowled at me – 'will this supposed "wonder drug" of yours cure the dreadful pain in my sixth, seventh and eighth tentacles? I mean it's EXCRUCIATING when I have to do something strenuous, like lift a piece of paper or stick a stamp on an envelope.

But the doctor doesn't listen to me. **Oh, dear me, no!** She just goes on and on about psycho-something-or-other. If you want to know what I think—'

I was about to engage my *'tune-Delores-out filter'* when the newcomer began to speak.

'Would you hold that fascinating thought for a second, Delores dear?' she said. And then, turning to me, she **smiled broadly** and added, 'I'm sorry, did you mention something about an IDV being parked badly?'

I didn't reply immediately. And when I finally did all I could manage to say was, 'Teeth.'

Which may sound a bit stupid. But in my defence I was completely **transfixed** by her smile. It was very, very wide and seemed to contain about as many teeth as **a very large dental museum.**

MON-MED

Chapter 3

'**O**h dear!' said the toothy monster with a laugh. 'Has my naughty IVAN parked in the wrong place again?' She held out her hand. *Her nails were beautifully manicured,*  but looked sharp enough to open a can of beans.

I shook it very, very carefully.

'I'm so sorry – how rude of me,' she added. 'My name is—'

'Ms Diagnosiz!' the doctor's loud voice boomed across the surgery as she emerged from the door to the basement garage. 'As I live and – occasionally – breathe! How on earth are you? **I haven't seen you since that food poisoning conference on Mushroom Island.** Do come straight through to my office. You too, Ozzy.'

I sighed. I had been hoping that I could go up to the swamp-spa treatment room and wash Lionel's boil goo out of my trousers. As we walked away a disgruntled Delores called out, 'Oh, I see! Just ignore me and my tentacle pain, then. And I suppose you'll be wanting some *tea and biscuits!*'

'BISCUITS!' cried the doctor. **'Marvellous idea!** And none of those cheap ones with nails in them. Break out the special biscuit tin.' She quickly closed the door on any further moaning and turned to me. 'Ozzy, allow me to introduce Ms Diagnosiz. **She is a sales rep from FANG-PHARMA Medical Supplies Inc.** They make—'

'Wunda-Wipes, Claw-Rotnot and No-Fungontung!' I interrupted proudly. I'd been brushing up on my monster medicines recently and remembered FANG-PHARMA because of their reassuring corporate motto:

FANG-PHARMA Medical Supplies
MUCH SAFER THAN LAST YEAR

The doctor sat down behind her desk and I took a chair, letting out an embarrassing squelch as I did so. But no one commented, as embarrassing **squelches** are pretty common in the surgery.

'Oh, I'm not working for them any more,' Ms Diagnosiz trilled. 'I'm at **MON-MED** pharmaceuticals now.'

She placed her shiny briefcase on the doctor's desk. Then, after a quick struggle with the locks (due to her tiny arms and big nails), she offered me a business card.

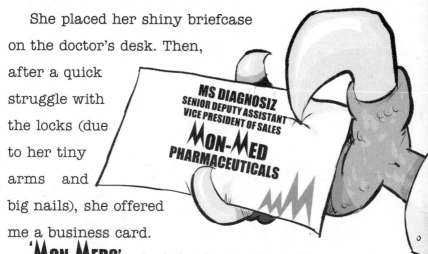

MS DIAGNOSIZ
SENIOR DEPUTY ASSISTANT
VICE PRESIDENT OF SALES
MON-MED
PHARMACEUTICALS

'**MON-MED?**' asked the doctor. One of her ears wiggled in suspicion. (FYI: One ear wiggling = mild suspicion. Two = total disbelief.) 'Didn't they have an **enormous scandal with their tentacle ointment** causing that—?'

'Oh, that's all in the past now,' said Ms Diagnosiz waving one tiny arm dismissively. 'They had a complete shake-up after the previous management team were convicted and **dropped into a volcano.**'

Ms Diagnosiz gave a tinkling laugh as she took out a very expensive-looking shiny packet from the case. It was embossed with a snazzy letter 'F' on it. She opened it, tossed the packet into a nearby waste bin and pulled out a small bottle.

33

'Now, Annie, the reason I'm here is this little wonder.' She held the bottle up to the light. It contained a thin, green, slimy liquid that glowed ever so slightly in a way that liquids probably shouldn't. *It's called* **FIXITALL** *and it will instantly cure any of over three hundred major and minor monster illnesses!*

Ms Diagnosiz smiled brightly, before adding, 'And associated Thing complaints.'

I looked at the bottle dubiously. 'Can it heal giant-squid bites?' I was thinking about poor Simon Salamander in the waiting room.

'Of course!' answered the toothy sales rep smoothly. 'It's also available as a *handy tube of* **extra-gloopy slime** *ointment.*' She pulled a sample from her briefcase and tossed it to me.

'What about **severe sunburn?**' asked the doctor excitedly. 'We always have dreadful problems with vampires who forget to put on their factor one thousand sun cream on a nice day.'

'Oh yes, indeed!' Ms Diagnosiz went on. '**FIXITALL** will cure all major monster skin conditions including – but not limited to – **crustacea-irritata, scratchy-scab, arachnid-acne and werewolf silver blisters.**'

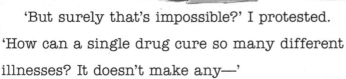

'But surely that's impossible?' I protested. 'How can a single drug cure so many different illnesses? It doesn't make any—'

Ms Diagnosiz reached for another box, and happened to knock me off my chair and into a **potted carnivorous shrub** in the process.

As I tried to extract myself without being bitten, she handed a glossy promotional leaflet to the doctor.

The doctor looked at it eagerly and asked, 'So how does it work, then?'

'Now, now, you know I can't possibly tell you that, Annie!' cried Ms Diagnosiz. 'It's all very hush-hush.' But then she leaned in conspiratorially and whispered, 'What I can tell you, though, is that **MON-MED**'s top scientist has made an *incredible breakthrough in Spaghetto-Genetics.* I don't want to say too much, but it may well be that soon **MON-MED** will be able to cure almost every monster illness!'

I looked between the two of them in confusion. 'Spaghetto-Genetics? What's that?'

'It's the monster genetic code.' The doctor sighed in exasperation and looked at me with **eyes full of disappointment.** 'It was in your reading *homework*⭐ for last week – along with some of the complications caused by head transplants and treatment for **babble-jaw syndrome.** You'll have to catch up later, in your own time,' she added crossly. 'Right now, I want to see this universal cure in action!'

I was just about to explain that I'd been helping babysit my monstrous little sister last week, and homework had been tricky because I had been busy dodging objects thrown by her and **cleaning up the various bodily fluids she deposited without warning** around the house. But at that moment Delores barged through the door. She was carrying a tray filled with cups of steaming, **fizzing bile tea** and a plate of scary-looking biscuits. She plonked it noisily down on the table right beside Ms Diagnosiz's open briefcase.

'Is this it, then?' she asked, snatching the bottle of **FIXITALL** from the T. Rex. 'This is the universal cure that'll fix my aching tentacle cramps?'

And before Ms Diagnosiz could stop her, the receptionist had opened the bottle of **FIXITALL** and glugged the slimy gloop down as if it were a mug of cold bile tea.

Now this may sound like a **shockingly dangerous** thing to do, but then you've never seen the contents of Delores's side of the office fridge.

'I don't feel any different,' she said after a pause. 'How long does it take this stuff to—'

But she was unable to finish the sentence. An annoying *whine* had suddenly filled the room and for a moment I thought a bee was trapped in her hair. But then I realized the sound was actually coming from somewhere **inside Delores's left nostril.**

'Is this sort of thing normal with **FIXITALL?**' the doctor asked Ms Diagnosiz with interest.

The saleswoman smiled and nodded. 'Oh yes,' she said. 'Always the left nostril. *Quite normal.* And, as you can see, it's quickly followed by the smoke.'

'The smoke?' asked Delores, concern creeping into her voice. I noticed there were *indeed wisps of blue and green smoke* starting to pulse from her ears. It looked as if her brain had taken up pipe-smoking.

I started to back away, just in case the receptionist was actually about to explode. Because even though **I hadn't yet seen an entire monster explode,** much weirder things have happened to me in the last three weeks.

I took cover behind the swamp-water dispenser, which is nice and heavy, so I figured it might offer some protection in the event of Delores suddenly going **BOOM!**

A FEW TINY SIDE-EFFECTS

Chapter 4

Ms Diagnosiz, however, seemed unconcerned about the possibility of an explosion.

'Patients may be alarmed at first,' she explained, 'by the **nasal whining** and *ear smoke*. But they're a vital indicator to the medical professional that **FIXITALL** slime is **working**.'

'Jolly useful,' agreed the doctor. 'And is the right eyeball revolving clockwise normal too?'

'Yes,' said Ms Diagnosiz. 'And you'll notice that the left one is moving anti-clockwise at the same time. She is entering the final treatment phase now. But don't worry. **It'll all be over any second** . . .' She looked down at her very expensive bejewelled watch. 'In fact, right about . . . **now!**'

Exactly on cue, both eyes stopped spinning. (Which was just as well as I was starting to feel **a bit dizzy.**)

'Are you all right, Delores?' I asked the grumpy receptionist nervously, getting ready to dodge her nearest tentacles or suffer some particularly cutting remark about my hair.

To my **astonishment,** she smiled pleasantly back at me.*

I shuddered.

'Are you all right?' I repeated, cautiously emerging from behind the crusty water dispenser.

'All right?' She beamed.

* The words 'Delores', 'smiled' and 'pleasant' are an unnatural combination to find in any one sentence. In fact, I'd only ever seen the receptionist smile once before. And that had been as unsettling an experience as my grandma's 'special' vegetarian chilli.

'Oh yes, Ozzy! I'm as right as rain, sweetie! **My dreadful tentacle cramp is completely gone!** And I feel simply . . .' She stretched her sixth, seventh and eighth tentacles out and twined them around each other as if they were newborn puppies wriggling in a basket. 'OOOOOOOH! What's the word . . .? *Lovely! I haven't felt this flexible since I was young and starring in Madam Squidling's dancing-tentacle troupe.'*

Then, to my utter horror, she laughed girlishly and actually tossed her hair like a pony.

UGH!

'What an extraordinary achievement!' cried the monster doctor. 'A universal cure? Why, this could be even more **significant** than the discovery of Head Massage Therapy.'

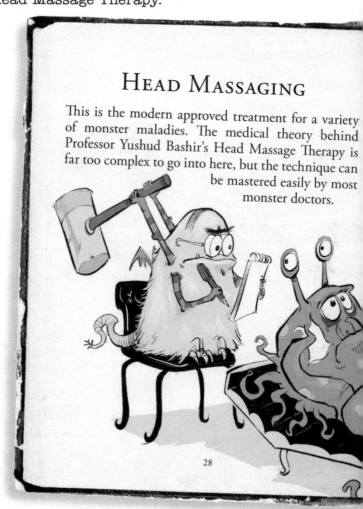

HEAD MASSAGING

This is the modern approved treatment for a variety of monster maladies. The medical theory behind Professor Yushud Bashir's Head Massage Therapy is far too complex to go into here, but the technique can be mastered easily by most monster doctors.

28

In short, the patient is seated in a comfortable chair while the therapist approaches them from behind with a large massage hammer.
The patient is then struck repeatedly on the head.

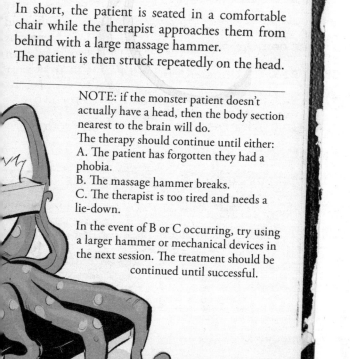

NOTE: if the monster patient doesn't actually have a head, then the body section nearest to the brain will do.
The therapy should continue until either:
A. The patient has forgotten they had a phobia.
B. The massage hammer breaks.
C. The therapist is too tired and needs a lie-down.

In the event of B or C occurring, try using a larger hammer or mechanical devices in the next session. The treatment should be continued until successful.

I still wasn't sure. A **universal cure** sounded a bit like **a shortcut** to me. And in my experience shortcuts didn't work – especially when Dad was driving, as they always seemed to end up with us in the *wrong country,* or having to be pulled out of the canal. But the doctor didn't seem to be worried at all.

'A universal cure for monster illness . . .' she said dreamily. 'That might mean I can start thinking about taking it a bit easier. What with Ozzy's studies coming along so nicely, perhaps I could finally go part-time. *Spend more time on my hobbies.* It's been decades since I did any still-life boil painting. And the campaign to reintroduce mammoth racing has stalled recently . . .'

'Well, now's your chance to try it,' said Ms Diagnosiz quickly. '**MON-MED** is giving *an exclusive* list of monster doctors and celebrities a chance to try **FIXITALL** before it goes on general release.'

The doctor positively beamed. 'Well, you can count us in!'

'Excellent!' said Ms Diagnosiz, once again showing off all her teeth as she rummaged around in her briefcase. 'There are just a couple of tiny things I need from you. Firstly, there's the small **administration fee** of eight hundred Karloffs.'

'Eight hundred Karloffs!' I blurted. You can buy a three-course dinner for two at **The Battered Squid chippy** – including a large plate of dread and butter – for less than one Karloff.

'Oh, it's only money, Ozzy!' chided the monster doctor. 'What's the other thing, Ms Diagnosiz?'

The saleswoman produced a legal form.

'I just need your signature here –' she pointed with one extremely sharp claw – '**here, and** ... **here!** It's just the standard **legal stuff** about **side-effects**, patients' legs **falling off**, et cetera.'

'Er . . . should **MON-MED** really be selling medicine that makes patients' limbs fall off?' I asked. But for some reason the doctor, Ms Diagnosiz and even Delores all began to laugh.

'BAN a medicine because of a few side-effects?' exclaimed the doctor, wiping the tears from her eyes. 'Oh dear. Whatever next? There's **nothing wrong** with a few side-effects, Ozzy. All the really useful monster medicines have side-effects. Even No-Fungontung causes **large horns to suddenly sprout from inappropriate parts of the body.** But a few dozen extra horns is a price worth paying to have a nice slimy tongue, isn't it?'

I wasn't sure.

The doctor turned to the very eager-looking Ms Diagnosiz. 'I'll take the lot!' she said enthusiastically.

Ten minutes later Ms Diagnosiz was driving away in her shiny black car. There was a **large pile** of **FIXITALL** packets on Delores's counter and an even larger hole in the doctor's wallet.

'Hand these out to **any patient** that wants them, Ozzy,' said the doctor. 'And then please get yourself cleaned up. **You're trailing boil pus all around the surgery.'** She was right. The contents of Lionel's nasal boil had been slowly sliding down all morning and was now starting to congeal unpleasantly in the **underpants region.**

As I dispensed the **FIXITALL** slime, not a single monster seemed to share my worries about potential side-effects. Simon Salamander, both the Vlads, Mrs Graves, Oswalt Sadbottom and every other **sickly patient** gratefully took a bottle of the slimy 'universal cure' and scurried off home.

In a few minutes the **FIXITALL** was all gone and the surgery was empty, save for the doctor, me, an **unnaturally happy Delores** and an **unnaturally grumpy Morty.** (Even a wonder drug couldn't stitch a zombie back together.)

'Do you need my help stitching Morty back together before I get cleaned up?' I asked the doctor.

Delores laughed and said, 'Don't you worry yourself, Ozzy. I'll help the doctor.' The idea of Delores actually volunteering to help is about as unlikely as hearing that a **giant asteroid,** which was about to wipe out all life on Earth, has just bounced harmlessly off **Milton Keynes**.

I excused myself from the weirdness and **squelched** out of the room. It was going to take some time to get used to 'nice' Delores. (And even longer to get the disturbing mental image of her dancing out of my brain.)

But luckily I had something wonderful to look forward to. I was about to have the *finest shower in the known universe.*

SPURTIE

Chapter 5

The swamp-spa treatment room on the third floor of the surgery is not really safe for humans. And by 'not really safe for' I mean 'extremely dangerous for'.

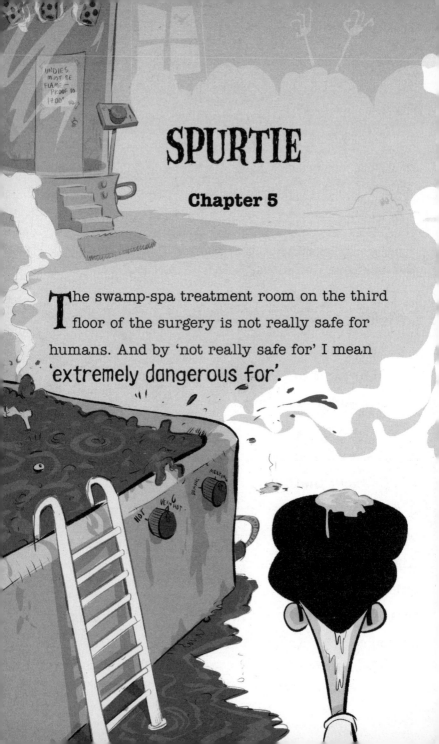

It was built to treat monsters
whose natural environment can
best be described as damp and **fetid.**
For instance, there is a swamp-gas
sauna booth that is best avoided
if you are stubbornly attached
to human ideals like breathing.
And there's a brand-new
quicksand jacuzzi that is very useful for
treating **serious troll skin conditions** – as long
as you're not bothered about the possibility of
suddenly **bursting** into flames.

55

Still, despite this, the spa contains two things that are very *special to me.*

The first is my locker. This is where I keep changes of **clean clothing**. (As you may have noticed being a trainee monster doctor can be an extremely messy, slimy business.)

The second is Spurtie.

Spurtie is the **shower snake.**

I mean, electric showers, power showers and even those fancy home spas with the **nozzles** that squirt water into places you weren't really expecting are all fine, but for the ultimate shower experience you really, really, REALLY need to have a shower snake.

Extract from Archibald Flim's THE ODDER PLACE: A Traveller's Guide to the Stranger Bits of Dimension 3.71:

The inhabitants of dimension 3.71 are the shower snakes of Fountane Lake. Their bodies comprise of a long wriggly tube with a hole at each end. They spend their days sucking filthy swamp water in (via the end without eyes) and then spraying it out (via the end with eyes). Amazingly, the water exits their body sparklingly clean, nicely warm and with a natural soapy additive that smells of vanilla.

No one knows why they do this.

But we should be eternally grateful that they do.

I opened the door to the spa – remembering to step over the hydrochloric acid footbath – and began to undress. One by one, I dropped the soiled clothes into the open and eager mouth of the laundry monster.

The hungry creature burped, said, **'Fank yoo vewy much!'** and began to greedily suck all the dirt and boil pus off my clothes. **They'd be nice and clean-ish sometime tomorrow.** Though it would probably hang on to one of my socks as payment.

I opened the door to the shower cubicle.

'Good morning, Spurtie,' I said to the shower snake as he uncoiled from his perch. **Spurtie was about six feet long,** as thick as a vacuum cleaner cord and was striped bright blue and orange.

'GOOOD MOORNING, OOZEEE!' he replied. **'YOO WONNN A WOSHHHH?'** Shower snakes find it very hard to make anything other than vowel sounds because their mouths are shaped like a nozzle.

'Yes, please!' I replied eagerly as Spurtie dipped his tail (the end without eyes) into the **sewage outlet.** 'And is there any chance you could make it a little bit more gentle this ti—' But before I could finish speaking the shower snake was enthusiastically *blasting* me with its fire-hose jet of warm, sweet-smelling soapy water.

It was bliss!

Ten minutes later I was towelled off, wearing clean clothes and back downstairs in the deserted surgery. Since no one was about and all my chores for the day were done — **bile leeches fed, nasal worms safely locked up, toe and horn clippers sharpened** — I decided to have a quick read about Spaghetto-Genetics.

I made myself a nice cup of *hot sluggaccino,* grabbed a plate of mostly human-safe biscuits and settled down in the waiting room with a copy of *TANGLED UP IN YOU — A Basic Primer on Monster Spaghetto-Genetics.*

Introduction
What is Spaghetto-Genetics?

We monsters come in an
extraordinary variety of
shapes and sizes. From the
two-inch long nasal worm
to the fifteen-thousand ton
maxocolossosaurapod.
From the slippery lagoon lizard
to the dry and dusty Saharan
sponge worm.

Nasal worm

Maxocolossosaurapod

Over the centuries many theories have
been put forward to try to explain
this extraordinary diversity – which is
especially extraordinary when compared
to other creatures like human beings
and monkeys, who only come
in one rather boring shape.

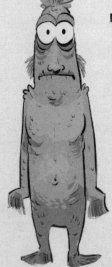

Lagoon lizard

Saharan sponge worm

Human being
(Tail optional)

Could this brilliantly diverse range be something to do with the colour of underwear your monster ancestors wore? Could it be caused by eating too much rusty metal, or maybe the wrong kind of people?

Tentaclio Spaghetti

There was no answer. That is, until monster doctor Tentaclio Spaghetti discovered that every single cell in a monster's body contains hundreds of intertwined strands of genetic code. We now call this code DNA (Dexy-Noodleclaic-Acid) or, more commonly, Spaghetto-Genetics. And it's the very complexity of this DNA that allows for the amazing physical diversity of monsters. Tentaclio was awarded the Trollsmell Prize for monster cleverness in 1921.

I was just about to read the first chapter when I was disturbed by the sound of raised voices coming from the street outside. Then someone began **hammering on the front door.**

Whoever it was did not sound happy.

'DOCTOR!' I yelled.

She instantly appeared with her shirt sleeves rolled up, carrying something wriggling. 'What's going on?' she said, handing me a large needle, some thread and Morty's still-wriggling left hand. She grabbed the door handle and **flung the door open** to reveal an angry mob of the surgery's patients.

MUSTARD CREAMS

Chapter 6

'**SIDE-EFFECTS!**' slobbered Simon Salamander. **'Is that what you call this?'** He held up three of his arms for the doctor to inspect. I was amazed – the bite marks were gone! He was completely healed.

Unfortunately, his **healed skin** was now a rather **unpleasant combination** of yellow, pink and mauve vertical stripes. 'It's been like this since I took that **stupid slime** you prescribed!' he complained. 'And it's not just me that's been affected. **Look at that poor monster!**' He pointed across Lovecraft Avenue at Oswalt Sadbottom, a very shy ogre the doctor was treating for his nerves. Oswalt seemed to be unable to reach the surgery because his right leg had shrunk to **half the length of the left.** The poor ogre was finding it almost impossible to walk in anything other than a circle.

Vlad and Vladness the vampires appeared suddenly from behind us, making the doctor and I jump. (How did they do that?) I noticed they were both carrying shopping bags full of *fresh salad.* And Vlad was gnawing like a beaver on a stick of celery.

'**Help us, doktor!**' pleaded Vlad. 'Ever since ve drank **zat disguzting zlime of yours,** ze sight of blood makes my vife and I feel very queasy.'

'Now all ve can do,' added Vladness, tossing radishes into her mouth as if they were *chocolate bonbons,* 'iz eat zis awful salad. But ve cannot live like zis. What kind of monster eats just vegetables?'

As they spoke, other monsters pressed in on the doctor, also demanding answers. And even more were heading up Lovecraft Avenue towards us.

'I don't understand,' said the doctor. 'It must be the **FIXITALL. But surely no single medicine can have so many bizarre side-effects?**'

'We didn't actually read the side-effects leaflet, though, did we?' I said.

The doctor gave me the same blank look my **grandpa**  does when I try to explain a **really modern invention, like the internet or the indoor toilet.**

'What side-effects leaflet?' she asked.

I ran to the doctor's office and retrieved the **FIXITALL** packet from the waste bin. On the way back outside, I extracted the **thick folded paper leaflet** and passed it to the doctor. I got the distinct impression that it was the first time in her long life that she had ever seen such a leaflet.

'Are you seriously telling me there's a complete list of side-effects inside every packet of monster medicine ever produced?'

I nodded.

'Well, I'll be blowed!' the doctor said. 'I always thought that bit of paper was in there for padding! What will they think of next, eh?

I suppose we'd better read it.'

So we read it.

It was a very long list.

Here is a short extract.

PAGE 1

MM MON-MED PHARMACEUTICALS

FIXITALL SIDE-EFFECTS (MILD)

Dry eyes.
Watery eyes.
Extra eyes.
Stiffness.
Floppiness.
Extreme dizziness leading to extreme falling over.
Skin rashes consisting of spots, stripes, tweed, plaid, herringbone, leopard, tiger, ocelot and, in some severe cases, obscure Scottish tartans.
Individual leg lengths may differ from one day to the next.

Putting on weight – including skin.
Unnatural niceness.
Unexplained, rapidly growing boils.
Unexpected and unwanted air in undesirable places.
Strange appetites. (Manure, corrugated steel, pilchards (including canned), sliced white supermarket bread, radioactive isotopes and, in some severe cases, salad.)
Sudden unexplained fluency in Classical Japanese.

And it went on and on. There were **seventeen** more pages of symptoms. And these were only the mild ones!

I looked up and spotted Gordon the ghoul
approaching, shouting something incompre-
hensible in what I assumed was *Classical
Japanese.* Melisssa Medusa was slithering up
the pavement, a furious look on her face and her
snake hair all **stiff and erect like a reptilian
pincushion.** Even the normally polite and very
neat skeleton, Mrs Graves, was heading for us,

dragging her bony little dog, Tibia, behind her. She looked as if she'd put on some skin, and she didn't look very happy about it.

It was turning into an **ugly crowd.** (Well, uglier than usual, anyway.) And if we didn't do something quickly we might end up with another **patient riot** on our hands. But luckily one thing living with my family has taught me is that there is a **sure-fire way of nipping any potential riot in the bud.**

Tea and biscuits.

'Delores!' I called out cheerily. 'I think it's time to make a nice pot of bile tea for everyone and –' I paused dramatically – 'perhaps break out the special biscuit tin.'

The monster crowd instantly went very still.

Delores's special biscuit tin was **legendary** among the doctor's patients. Many had heard of it, but few had ever been lucky enough to be granted a glimpse of its contents.

'*What a lovely idea!*' Delores beamed. (Which was **REALLY** weird, as she would normally have removed a limb from anyone who touched her special biscuit tin.) 'Everyone follow me!' She slithered happily off towards the kitchen while *gaily whistling a creepy monster music-hall tune.*

But it worked.

Vladness said, 'Zat vud be lovely! I vunder if she has any of thoze **hairy baldis** you like, Vlad?' And before long the monsters were following Delores inside to the waiting room, arguing about which biscuits were the best: mustard creams, chocolate indigestives or whinger snaps.

Biscuits – as always – had averted a **riot.**

The doctor smiled reassuringly at the patients as she dragged me towards her office.

She closed the door and hissed, 'This is terrible! I've never seen so many different side-effects before! We've got to find out what is going on before someone gets really annoyed and **eats us.**'

'Can you call someone at **MON-MED?**' I asked.

'Another brilliant idea, Nurse Ozzy!' she exclaimed. **'There's bound to be a perfectly natural explanation as to why a pharmaceutical sales rep would sell me a patently dangerous medicine.'**

I didn't say anything.

She pulled out her monster mobile and began dialling. Someone answered, and the doctor put it on speaker.

But it was only the answerphone.

A smug voice began to recite,

'You have reached **MON-MED** pharmaceuticals. Unfortunately we have ceased trading due to ongoing legal action. If you experience any unusual or dangerous medical issues we suggest you contact *a fully qualified monster doctor*. Failing that, you could lie down in a nice dark box. Or, if you don't have a box handy, you could just hang up now. We would also like to take this opportunity to thank you for being a customer of **MON-MED** pharmaceuticals and please remember, your sickness was always very important to us.'

And with that the line went dead.

MALPRACTICE

Chapter 7

'**A**h,' said the doctor as she replaced the phone receiver. '**This is bad. Very bad.**'

'I thought you said a few side-effects were OK in monster medicine,' I said.

'Oh, Ozzy!' she exclaimed. 'This isn't the same thing at all. It's not like giving monster aspirin to a Thing,* or giving a mother a baby with the wrong number of heads! No, this is SERIOUS! **This is a FOUR M EMERGENCY!**'

Now, by an amazing coincidence, I knew exactly what the doctor was referring to. You see, my **homework** the previous evening had been to read Dr Yuri Tooblaym's popular book:

OOPS! THAT WASN'T SUPPOSED TO HAPPEN!
A Beginner's Guide to Monster Medical Malpractice.

> * Monsters and things are very different. Monsters are born weird. Things are made weird by events.

MULTIPLE MONSTER MEDICINE MALPRACTICES

Giving a patient the wrong (or dangerous) medicine is quite normal and not actually that serious if you have good enough malpractice insurance. Unfortunately, even this won't protect a doctor who has dosed multiple patients. If this happens, there are three main options available to the monster doctor:

FLEE.
Dimension 2.6 has a no-extradition policy with the 'civilized' monster universe – and it has some lovely red-hot swampside resorts.

BLAME YOUR ASSISTANT.
This is why I personally recommend hiring one or more stupid assistants. It is at times like these that they really come into their own.

TRY TO FIX THE PROBLEM.
This will give you the rosy glow of having done the right thing. But it has some obvious downsides: expensive court cases, prison, being eaten, etc.

'But what are we supposed to do?' I asked. 'If **MON-MED** pharmaceuticals has *gone bust*, then where are we going to find a *cure* for **FIXITALL?** It's not as if we can just break into their top-secret research lab, find out how **FIXITALL** works and then try to make a cure oursel—'

I stopped talking, realizing that the doctor was staring at me very oddly. Was she considering Dr Yuri Tooblaym's tempting option number two? But

before I could make a break for the surgery's exit the doctor had seized me in her **orangutan arms.** She was laughing like a hyena who's had eight double espressos.

'YEEGHR CRUSHING ME!' I gasped.

She let me go. 'I'm sorry. I forget how delicate you are.' She was still beaming at me, though. 'You're such a little marvel, Ozzy! One moment I'm staring at your strange dorsal nasal appendage and thinking, **Annie, why did you hire this human assistant? The poor thing is less intelligent than a recently revived zombie slug.'**

That was nice to know.

'But then the next moment you come out with a **completely brilliant** plan like that!' She opened a drawer in her desk and flung the glossy **MON-MED** pharmaceuticals brochure at me. 'See if you can find the address for the **MON-MED** head office in there.'

It was on the inside back page. Right beside one of those inter-dimensional 'WE ARE HERE' maps that are about as easy to understand as one of my little sister's drawings on the fridge door. Still, Bruce would understand it.

'But how are we going to get in?' I asked.

'Don't fret,' she replied, rummaging around in the bottomless drawer of her desk. **'THIS** will get us inside.' She produced *a tube that was roughly the size of a rolled-up boy-band poster.* One end was painted green and the other was red. The red end was labelled very clearly with a large arrow and the words:

THIS END TOWARDS PATIENT

'Therapy bazooka,' she explained, seeing my confused look. 'Incredibly useful for advanced *head-massaging therapies,* un-blocking the surgery's drains and opening stubborn doors.'

'But surely breaking into the **MON-MED top-secret research lab** must be dangerous,' I said in a feeble attempt to avoid the embarrassment of having my parents come and bail me out of monster jail. 'Won't they have security guards with **large teeth or fiery breath?'**

The doctor dismissed my concerns. 'We mustn't let little things like –' she made air quotes – 'being **"badly bitten"** or **"burned to a crisp"** get in the way of helping poorly monsters, Ozzy!'

'Can't we?' I said with some concern. 'Why ever not?'

She drew herself **up to her full height** – which, even counting those extra storeys of hair, isn't as tall as me.

'CURA OMNIA, Ozzy!' she insisted, quoting the monster doctor's motto to me. **'HEAL ANYTHING!** We are **highly trained** monster doctors and it is our **duty** to help any monsters who are ill – especially if we caused that illness! Come!'

She jabbed a button on the **intercom** marked GARAGE.

'We have sick patients to cure.'

There was an answer from the garage. The speaker emitted a subsonic **grumble** that made all the ornaments fall off the doctor's desk.

'Hello, Lance –' the doctor paused as the desk began to shake again. Then she said, 'Oh dear! I'm sorry! **I didn't realize you were in the bath. But this is an emergency.** Would you mind terribly putting Bruce on, please?'

There was the sound of loud **revving** as Lance shouted for Bruce to pick up the phone.

Bruce replied with a high-pitched screech that would have made my dog Piglet feel an inexplicable urge to go and round up some sheep. Then the **small monitor** beside the **phone** lit up with Bruce's familiarly unfriendly font.

> WHAT DO YOU WANT?
> IT'S MY AFTERNOON OFF.

'I know, I know,' said the doctor. 'And I'll make it up to you later. But right now we have an emergency and I thought you might *appreciate*

the chance to do something exciting for a change? Something like *breaking* into **MON-MED** pharmaceuticals' top-secret research lab.'

There was a second – even higher-pitched – screech from the phone.

The doctor winced and held the receiver a safe distance from her pointy ears. And I knew that *somewhere out in the real world* Piglet was running round and round in circles looking for sheep.

'I assume that's a "yes",' said the doctor.

OFF THE TELLY

Chapter 8

Five minutes later, after another dizzyingly terrifying journey through inter-dimensional space, we were back in reality and *rolling along a long, smooth driveway.* It wound through an

enormous spread of manicured lawn towards a strange structure that I assumed was **MON-MED** headquarters. I assumed this because it seemed highly unlikely that anyone else would have had the money (or the bad taste) to **build a seven hundred and fifty foot tall tower out of glass and gleaming chrome**, in the shape of an **enormous** hypodermic syringe.

Lance screeched up to the lobby and **reverse-parked** (rather showily) in the spot reserved for the **VICE PRESIDENT WITH THE SECOND-LARGEST HEAD.**

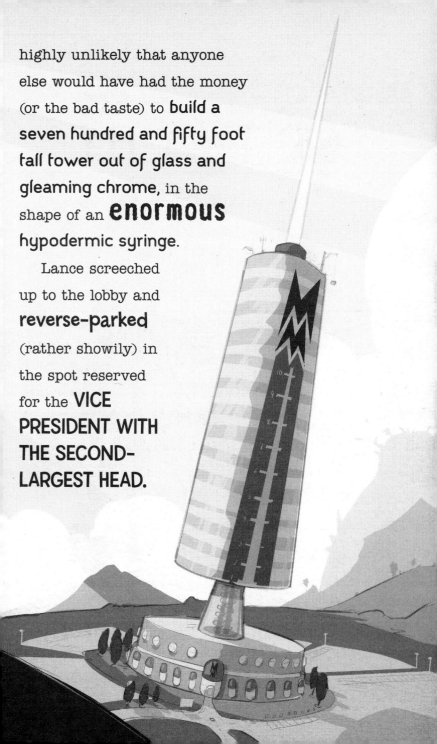

The doctor and I eagerly leaped out, to find – as expected – that the whole place was completely **boarded** up.

Posters with large red type announced:

MON-MED REGRETS TO INFORM VISITORS THAT OUR OFFICES ARE CLOSED UNTIL FURTHER NOTICE.
PLEASE FEEL FREE TO LEAVE IMMEDIATELY. OR STAY TO BE SAVAGED AND BURNED BY OUR SECURITY CONTRACTOR.
THANK YOU.

I didn't like the sound of being 'savaged and burned', and mentioned my worry to the doctor.

'PAH!' she scoffed, retrieving the therapy bazooka from Lance's back seat. 'We'll be inside before any **sluggish five-tonne grottviler** can catch us.' She raised the bazooka to her shoulder and took aim at the entrance.

Her finger tightened on the **trigger.**

I closed my eyes, stuck my fingers in my ears and waited for the explosion.

BOOOOOOOOMMMMM!

The earth shook.

This was a bit odd. Did a *therapeutic* **rocket-launcher** really need to be that strong? But when I opened my eyes the door was still intact. The doctor hadn't even fired the **bazooka.**

'Did you hear that?' she asked.

'You mean the—' I began, but was interrupted by another earth-shaking tremor.

BOOOOOOOMMMMM!

But this time it was louder and closer.

'Is it an—?'

BOOOOOOOMMMMM!

My teeth rattled.

'. . . earthquake?' I asked.

BOOOOOOOMMMMM!

My fillings rattled.

BOOOOOOOMMMMM!

'Doctor?'

But she wasn't listening. Instead, she was staring rather rudely up past the top of my head. She had dropped the therapy bazooka and her hands were **clutched together** – almost in *prayer*. She wore an expression I had seen many times before on the faces of my friends. It's the one they get when they see someone *famous off the telly or the internet.* Someone who's incredibly good at applying lipstick or running around after various-sized balls.

'By the extremely **damp** dining rooms of Atlantis!' she cried. 'It's HIM! It's actually HIM!'

There was another

BOOOOOOOMMMM!

that was so close it felt as if someone had dropped an aircraft carrier right behind me. So I turned round, and my eyes immediately fell upon a hill that hadn't been there a minute ago.

Of course it wasn't actually a hill. Hills can't walk (most of the time) and aren't usually covered in armour-plated scales.

It was the **biggest monster** I had ever seen.

'Gorgonzilla!' whispered the doctor. She was

gazing up adoringly at two colossal legs, each as

tall and thick as the Leaning Tower of

Pisa. They supported a colossal body,

an equally colossal neck and a head *the*

size of a five-bedroom detached house.

The creature must have weighed five thousand

tonnes and was built as **solidly** as an office block.

Which made it slightly worrying that it appeared

to be swaying, as if it didn't quite have its balance.

**'MR
GORGONZILLA,
SIR!'** bellowed
the doctor. **'I'M
A HUGE FAN!
THOUGH NOT AS
HUGE AS YOU, OF
COURSE!'** She gave

an embarrassed laugh.

**'CAN I JUST SAY HOW
MUCH I LOVED YOU IN
FRIGHT OF THE BUMBLE-BOMBS?
I WAS THERE IN TOKYO BACK IN '68.**

THAT HEART-BREAKING DUET WITH CATERPILLEROID LITERALLY BROUGHT THE HOUSE DOWN.'

And most of the city too, I suspected. Gorgonzilla looked ponderously down towards the source of the noise. Buzzing around his head was a small cloud of media camera drones (which is quite normal for such a **huge monster celebrity**). One of them seemed to cause him to momentarily **lose his balance,** and he put an arm out to steady himself. Unfortunately, the nearest support was the hypodermic spire of the **MON-MED** building, which snapped off in his **scaly claw** like a breadstick. The media drones darted excitedly in for a closer look.

'He doesn't seem very steady on his feet,' I observed.

'Steady on his feet?' snorted the doctor. 'Have you never heard of Gorgonzilla? He's one of the most graceful dancers in *modern monster ballet!*'

'That's a *dancer?*' I asked disbelievingly.

'Oh, don't let that **crusty exterior** fool you,' the doctor gushed. 'Beneath his ten-foot-thick *armour plating beats the heart* of a *true artist.* I've been his biggest fan ever since – ugh, don't look now.' She scowled. 'But one of those **ghastly media parasites** has spotted us.' And, sure enough, one of the buzzing things had swooped down from the sky.

Up close, it looked like a cross between a small helicopter and a very large, fanged mosquito. It hovered a few feet away, wielding an impressive selection of **long-lensed TV cameras** and several **mobile phones**. It was wearing a bright orange vest with the words 'COLOSSAL-GOSSIP TV' emblazoned across it.

'No pictures!' buzzed the drone as it pointed to the therapy bazooka on the ground. *'COLLOSAL-GOSSIP* has an **exclusive contract** with Mr G's management team.

We're shooting a true-life behind-the-scenes all-access exposé of Mr G's comeback tour. No outside press allowed.'

'We're not press,' I explained. 'We're doctors – or at least the doctor is.'

'And this isn't a camera,' added the monster doctor. 'It's a therapy bazooka. Would you like me to **demonstrate** on you?'

The drone quickly backed off to a safe distance. 'My apologies!' it buzzed. 'Bizzi Fartangle at your service. Senior video correspondent for *COLOSSAL-GOSSIP TV.'*

Far above our heads, Gorgonzilla swayed alarmingly again, and Bizzi zoomed *several lenses* up at him.

'Ooops-a-daisy!' he said. 'He's been like this all morning. Ever since he drank that **slimy wonder** drug. Now, what was it called? FEXITALL . . .? FOXITALL . . .?'

The doctor and I exchanged a glance. **'FIXITALL,'** we said simultaneously.

'Oh! You know about that?' asked Bizzi. 'Then you must know that *lovely* Ms . . . whatshername.'

'Diagnosiz,' I said with a sinking heart.

'That's her,' said Bizzi, nodding. 'Well, she signed a contract with Mr G's management team to try out this *hush-hush* new wonder cure for his RSI.'

Repetitive Stomping Injury (RSI)

RSI is a painful condition that affects very large monsters, and even some giants who are unfortunate enough to have both large feet and anger-management issues.

It is caused by repeatedly standing on otherwise harmless objects like buses, houses, railway trains, office blocks and Lego. Over time, the crushing impact can damage the delicate bones of a large monster's feet.

Treatment:

- Rest.
- No stomping.
- Sensible shoes.
- Avoid stepping on military vehicles like tanks, or Lego.

79

'Anyway,' continued the drone, 'Mr G has been as dizzy as a *helicopter-harpy* ever since he drank a **tankerful** of **FIXITALL** this morning. We were on our way here to shoot a totally spontaneous confrontation scene between him and the **MON-MED** management team. But he seems to have taken a turn for the worse.'

The drone was right. The **gigantic colossosaur** was now swaying as badly as the final terrifying moments of a game of *Mega-Jenga.*

'Doctor!' I exclaimed, thinking back to the list of **FIXITALL** side-effects. 'The leaflet said "extreme dizziness leading to extreme falling over"! We need to get Gorgonzilla safely lying down before he **falls over** and **injures** himself – or takes out a nearby town.'

The doctor instantly took charge. She cupped her hands and bellowed up at the colossosaur, **'MR GORGONZILLA, SIR? YOU'RE HAVING A FUNNY TURN. I REALLY THINK YOU SHOULD HAVE A NICE SIT-DOWN.'**

I could see the dizzy monster trying ever so hard to focus on her. But the effort made him sway even more **alarmingly** than before.

> '**PERHAPS YOU COULD TAKE A SEAT ON THAT HILL OVER THER—**'

She never got to finish her sentence. Because at that very moment Gorgonzilla lost his **balance** completely. Five thousand tonnes of monster began to topple over like a *chimney demolition* gone badly wrong.

Bizzi Fartangle buzzed away to safety, his cameras **whirring** as he **barked** orders into his multiple phones. 'CAMERA SEVEN, close-up on the face! CAMERAS THREE TO FIVE, **don't miss any collateral devastation!** CAMERA SIX, switch to slow-mo!'

But I just stood there, frozen to the spot. My **brain** was completely occupied with the fact that I was about to become **very, very flat.**

Luckily, the doctor's lifetime experience of certain-death situations has left her **immune to panic.** She simply tutted, picked me up by the back of my trousers and scurried towards Lance. Her tiny legs were *moving so quickly* that they were as bLurry as a bad holiday photo.

'LANCE! OPEN YOUR DOORS!' she yelled.

The ambulance's passenger side door obediently flapped open and the doctor flung me through it like a **bowling ball.**

She managed to grab hold of Lance's wing mirror and, just as I hit the driver's side door, she yelled, **'DRIIIIVVVVE!'**

The ambulance immediately tore off across the parking lot as if someone had announced there was a *free oil bath* at the local garage.

But, unfortunately, he went in completely the wrong direction.

A DROPPED SAUSAGE

Chapter 9

Have you ever seen one of those films where an enormous building or crashing spaceship is collapsing and the hero idiot tries to get away by running TOWARDS the thing that is falling?

Well, that's exactly what Lance did.

(I told you he has no sense of direction.)

I grabbed his steering wheel and desperately turned it to the left.

Nothing happened.

'LANCE!' I shouted. 'GO LEFT!'

Nothing happened.

'LANCE!' the doctor yelled from where she hung from the wing mirror. 'GO RIGHT!'

The ambulance kept going straight ahead.

We were *racing* across the car park, but it was
no good. Gorgonzilla's five-thousand-tonne body
was now so close that it was **blotting** out the sun.
We were moments away from being completely
squished when something from the IDV **manual**

I had recently been reading popped into my head.

Extract from **YOU MAY FEEL SICK AT FIRST:**
IDV driving for beginners:

> The novice driver must always remember that IDVs cannot understand ordinary dimensional commands like LEFT, RIGHT, UP or DOWN. When issuing directions to your IDV, you should always use correct IDV terminology like 'Reverse-Wibble', 'Liftish' and 'Shim-wards'. And PLEASE take the time to learn the life-saving difference between a Wibble, a Wobble, a Wubble and a Wirbble.
>
> Failing that, just buy a BAT-NAV.

In the instant before we were crushed, I screamed a stream of complete nonsense.

'LANCE! DO A LIFTISH REVERSE-WIBBLE SHIM-WARDS!' The little ambulance's engine revved and my **stomach flipped** as if I'd just been ordered to perform a dance during school **assembly** in my most embarrassing underwear.

A second later, I realized with relief that Lance was a hundred yards away from the *collapsing* Gorgonzilla, and we were travelling in a safe direction.

Phew.

There was a PING! from Bruce. He was annoyed.

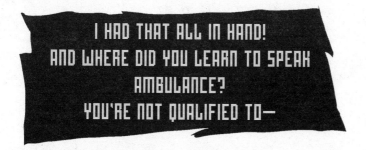

I HAD THAT ALL IN HAND!
AND WHERE DID YOU LEARN TO SPEAK
AMBULANCE?
YOU'RE NOT QUALIFIED TO—

Fortunately, he was drowned out by a two-hundred-decibel

CRASSSSHHHH!

Five thousand tonnes of Gorgonzilla collapsed on top of the **MON-MED** headquarters. The *gleaming* chrome-and-glass building was completely squished as clouds of dust, invoices, purchase orders and **customer complaints billowed** into the air.

They slowly floated back to earth, settling to reveal poor Gorgonzilla lying in the wreckage. He was sprawled on his back, colossal legs and arms **wriggling** in the air like a super-tanker-sized beetle. Bizzi Fartangle and her monster drones **swarmed** around, filming the whole incident.

The **MON-MED** headquarters was now as flat as my hair after ten minutes under Spurtie's shower.

The doctor jumped off Lance, *raced* over and **scrambled** up a small slope of **crushed executive** desks. I followed a bit more cautiously.

Finally, she reached the monster's **enormous** right eye. Gorgonzilla saw her and gave a sad little roar. And by 'little' I mean about as **loud** as a volcano erupting.

But the doctor seemed to understand what the colossosaur was saying. She pulled out her mobile phone and shouted, **'DO YOU HAVE THE NUMBER?'**

Gorgonzilla roared out what I assumed was a telephone number. Each roar made the **pile of debris** on which the doctor and I were perched tremble.

'Hello!' the doctor said into the phone. 'Is that COLOSSO-RECOVERY pick-up services?'

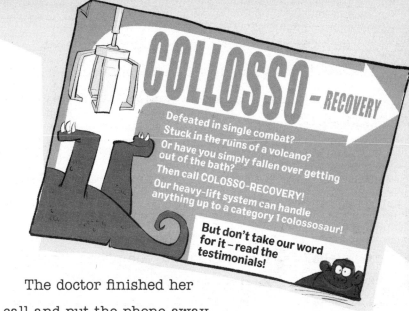

COLOSSO – RECOVERY

Defeated in single combat?
Stuck in the ruins of a volcano?
Or have you simply fallen over getting out of the bath?

Then call COLOSSO-RECOVERY!
Our heavy-lift system can handle anything up to a category 1 colossosaur!

But don't take our word for it – read the testimonials!

The doctor finished her call and put the phone away.

'THE DESPATCHER SAID THEY'LL BE HERE WITHIN THE HOUR, MR GORGONZILLA, SIR! SO YOU'D BEST STAY LYING DOWN TILL THEN. DON'T WORRY, THOUGH. MY ASSISTANT AND I ARE WORKING ON A CURE FOR FIXITALL AND WE EXPECT GREAT RESULTS VERY SOON!'

'Do we?' I whispered as the doctor and I **clambered** back through the ruins of the **MON-MED** building. 'I'm relieved you've got a plan B!'

'Of course I don't have a plan B!' the doctor snapped. 'We must work on your medicinal lying, Ozzy. It's very useful for keeping a patient's spirits up.' She *manoeuvred* around a pile of motivational posters. 'Somehow, we have to find a cure for that cursed slime medicine, and any answers that were in here –' she peevishly kicked the award for 'LEAST TOXIC LAXATIVE 1983–7' out of her way – 'are now as flat as sliced **wholemeal head**.'

'Surely you mean "wholemeal bread", I asked as we climbed back into Lance.

'What's "wholemeal bread"?' said the doctor **absent-mindedly** before adding, 'Home, please, Bruce.'

As Lance *rolled off across the car* park, I heard her mutter, 'Perhaps if Delores is still in a good mood she might let me run some experiments on her . . .'

But her musings were interrupted. For some reason, Lance began *madly swerving* back and forth. 'Oh! What on earth are you doing now, you **silly ambulance?**' cried the doctor. 'We don't have time for any more of your nonsense today!'

Lance screeched to a halt.

Then he *shot off again* in a completely different direction, changed his mind once more and began to spiral *round and round and round* in ever tighter and tighter handbrake turns. The doctor and I were thrown around like the ball bearing in a **vigorously** shaken can of spray paint.

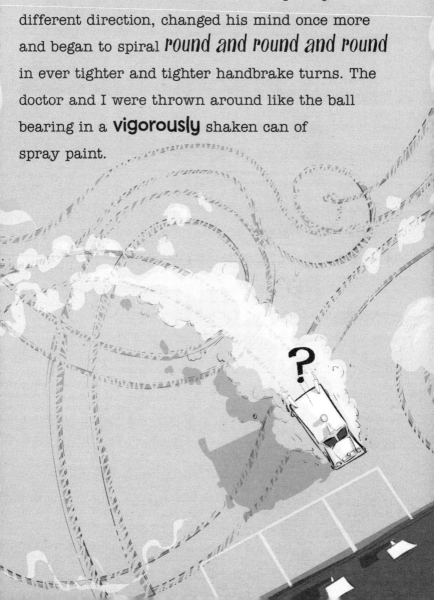

'**BRUCE!**' snapped the doctor from somewhere in the footwell. 'Tell Lance to stop this nonsense right now and take us straight home!'

DON'T LOOK AT ME!
I HAVEN'T A CLUE WHAT HE'S DOING.
IT'S QUITE FUNNY, THOUGH, ISN'T IT?

'I know what he's doing!' I cried excitedly as I tried to extract my left foot from the glovebox. 'He's behaving like **PIGLET!**'

'Are you delirious again, Ozzy?' asked the doctor. '**I did warn you against having one of Delores's toadstool vol-au-vents.**'

'No! It's not that. I just recognize Lance's behaviour.' I said this in as **un-smug** a way as I could manage (which was not very). 'He's searching for a smell. My dog Piglet goes back and forth across the kitchen floor looking for the EXACT spot where someone dropped a **sausage** two weeks before.'

I didn't add that when he finds the spot he spends the next three hours **licking the colour off the tiles.**

Lance came to a screeching, **tyre-burning** halt. The little ambulance's bonnet was pointing at a **nondescript patch of tarmac**. His engine purred proudly.

'What have you found, then, boy?' asked the doctor.

There was a loud **PING!** and Bruce's screen lit up.

HE SAYS HE KNOWS WHERE IT WENT.

'It?' I said.

THAT FANCY-PANTS CAR OF MS DIAGNOSIZ. OH, AND A LOAD OF FIXITALL TOO.

'She must have helped herself to all the remaining **FIXITALL** before the building was locked,' I exclaimed.

The doctor looked outraged. 'Come on, Ozzy!' she said. **'We have to find her before she can injure any more harmless monsters** like Gorgonzilla. Where is she, Bruce?'

ASTHMATIC PARROT

Chapter 10

A nd it literally was just round the corner.

Lance didn't even need to go inter-dimensional. He just drove for about a minute before turning into a **decrepit-looking trading** estate. A **totem sign** displayed the businesses unfortunate enough to have premises at such a **seedy** spot.

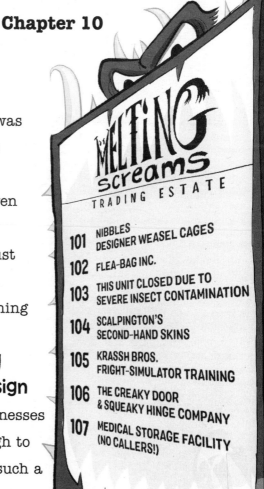

MELTING screams
TRADING ESTATE

101 NIBBLES DESIGNER WEASEL CAGES

102 FLEA-BAG INC.

103 THIS UNIT CLOSED DUE TO SEVERE INSECT CONTAMINATION

104 SCALPINGTON'S SECOND-HAND SKINS

105 KRASSH BROS. FRIGHT-SIMULATOR TRAINING

106 THE CREAKY DOOR & SQUEAKY HINGE COMPANY

107 MEDICAL STORAGE FACILITY (NO CALLERS!)

'Medical storage?' scoffed the doctor as Lance parked round the back by the *lock-up* garages and dumpsters. 'The cheek of that woman!'

She **strode round to the front of Unit 107** and took aim at the closed doorway with her therapy bazooka.

'WAIT!' I shouted.

The monster doctor does have this *regrettable* habit of trying to solve problems by hitting things with a **blunt object** or, failing that, the use of medicinal explosives.

'Let me guess,' said the doctor, giving me a disgusted look. 'You have a **revolutionary** way to find out what's going on inside without resorting to **explosives.**'

'Well, we could try looking through here first,'
I suggested. There was a small window further
along the wall that was mostly covered from the
inside with old newspapers. Luckily, one corner
(the **Daily Fang** sports page) had peeled away,
allowing just enough **space** for me to **peer** inside.

'Can you see Ms Diagnosiz?'
hissed the doctor.

'Yes,' I said.

She was sitting on a
chair at the side of the room, flicking
through holiday brochures for dimension 2.6.

'But there's something else . . .' I said
slowly. 'There's some kind of lab in there.'

'WHAT?' cried the doctor as she
squeezed in beside me. Together,
we took in the scene inside
Unit 107.

There was a **tall** glass **tank** surrounded by a maze of clear **tubes** and **glass chambers**. The tank reminded me of the home-made *aquarium* my grandad built in his first-floor flat at the nursing home. But instead of a collection of constantly **terrified fish,** this contraption contained a sort of bubbling, glowing, *gloopy green slime* that looked an awful lot like **FIXITALL.**

'By my auntie's fatally flammable flatulence!' exclaimed the doctor. 'She seems to be manufacturing **FIXITALL** in there!'

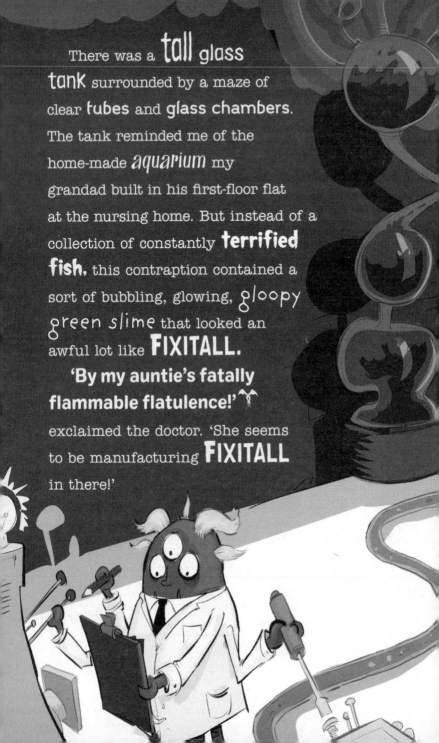

No sooner had she spoken than **two nimble little monsters** in spotless white lab coats appeared. They scurried across the complex assembly of glass and plastic, pausing only to **jot** down notes in a tiny notebook, tweak a valve or pull a lever.

Suddenly an automated voice began to count.
'TEN!'

Next to the tank, a hospital gurney I hadn't previously noticed was hoisted into an upright position.
'NINE!'

On the gurney was some kind of lizardy-fishy monster strapped (very tightly) on to it. The tiny lab-coated creatures began filling a very fearsome-looking syringe with the glowing slime from the tank. They pointed it straight at the strapped-down monster's arm.

'EIGHT!'

'What on earth are they doing?' asked the doctor.

'SEVEN!'

'Some kind of an experiment?' I suggested.

The doctor gasped. 'By **Frankenstein's** fatal folly!' cried the doctor. 'We have to save that poor monster!'

'SIX!'

A second later she was back on her feet by the doorway to Unit 107. Her face was bright blue with anger and the therapy bazooka was once again aimed right at the front door.

'FIVE!'

I just had time to stick my fingers in my ears before **she pulled the trigger.** There was a muffled **BANG** and the door turned into a thousand-piece jigsaw puzzle. As the shattered pieces hit the floor, the doctor charged inside.

'THREE!'

'STOP THIS!' she cried. 'WHATEVER "THIS" IS – AT ONCE!' The two tiny monsters were frozen in shock at the sight of her, so the doctor waved the therapy bazooka to emphasize the point. 'TWO!'

One of them sneezed in alarm, *yanked* open a valve and threw its hands in the air. 'ON—'

The countdown stopped. There was a loud gurgle and the contents of the syringe drained back into the *main tank.* A stunned Ms Diagnosiz hurriedly hid her holiday brochure and sprang to her feet. Her huge mouth opened in her **automatic** toothy smile.

'I can explain everything,' she began, but any 'explanation' was cut short by a **furious squawk** of anger behind us.

There was another monster in the room.

'Who are you?' a voice croaked. The doctor and I turned to find ourselves confronted by what looked like a five-thousand-year-old parrot. It was **wearing** a 'white' lab coat. (I say 'white' but it had seen more action than one of my baby sister's reusable eco-nappies.)

'What is the meaning of using a therapy bazooka on my front door?' the monster demanded, glaring angrily at us from beneath a rather obvious wig. 'And where on earth is Ms Diagnosiz going?'

We turned at the sound of running footsteps just in time to see Ms Diagnosiz's **tail** slipping out of the back door.

'Stop her!' cried the doctor.

I was about to give *chase* when the elderly avian croaked, **'Hold on a moment!'** His voice was as dry as that of an asthmatic parrot, and he was squinting up at the doctor through a pair of spectacles with glass thick enough for **submarine portholes.** 'I know you!' Then his gnarly old beak opened in what could have – in more sympathetic lighting – been considered a smile. 'Von Sichertall, isn't it? Why, I haven't seen you since you were nearly expelled from Sorebones College for **that incident with the blue whale and the bicycle rack!'**

The doctor lowered the therapy bazooka as recognition suddenly dawned.

'By my grandfather's aerodynamic bingo wings,' cried the doctor. **'Professor Peckham,** from the department of Spaghetto-Genetics! I'm sorry I didn't recognize you, sir. It's just you've grown so horribly old and horrendously wrinkly!'

'Ha ha!' cackled the elderly avian, before dissolving into a fit of coughing.

'Can we leave the college *reunion* till later?' I said with some frustration.

'Ms Diagnosiz is getting clean away!'

'Calm down, Ozzy,' said the doctor. 'Sometimes the villain does get away. After all, this isn't some **silly made-up story** – this is the real world of monster medicine.'

I was about to protest, but at that moment the professor finally regained his breath. 'It's charming of you to *drop in* to see your old lecturer, Von Sichertall. And perhaps we can *reminisce* later. But right now I am in the middle of a vital – I say **VITAL** – experiment.' He gestured to his two tiny assistants. 'Ms Tenement! Mr Nimby! We shall begin again!'

One of the tiny creatures picked up a clipboard, while the other *refilled the large syringe.*

The professor flicked a switch and Mr Nimby (or Ms Tenement) positioned the syringe over the monster in the gurney.

'Professor!' exclaimed the doctor. 'Surely you can't mean to keep **experimenting** with **FIXITALL?** You realize there are terrible side-effects?'

'I know all about the side-effects,' replied Professor Peckham, **absent-mindedly** twiddling a knob.

'So why do it, then?' asked the doctor.

'Because I asked him to,' interrupted the patient.

The professor waved to where the monster lay strapped on the gurney. 'Dr Von Sichertall,' he announced. *Allow me to introduce* my former assistant, Mr Gillman. Mr Gillman, this is Dr Von Sichertall and her nurse-monkey-thing.'

Charmed, said Mr Gillman, offering his webbed hand to us.

It was covered in maroon *tartan.*

'That's not right,' I said, studying the pattern. 'If I'm not mistaken, you're a *Swampus noir lagoonis* and should be covered in mucus-coated scales.' (I'd recently watched an old black-and-white documentary about his species on MonTube.)

'Quite!' snapped the professor irritably. 'As you can clearly see, Mr Gillman is suffering from very severe **FIXITALL** side-effects. Now, if we are **quite finished** with the formal introductions, perhaps the old fool that invented **FIXITALL** –' he **pushed a button on the control console** – 'can be allowed to get on with trying to CURE **FIXITALL!**'

There was a **loud clunk,** which was either the syringe *plunging* into Mr Gillman's tartan arm or the doctor and my jaws hitting the floor.

SUCH PROMISING RESULTS . . .

Chapter 11

'**Y**ou invented **FIXITALLL?**' asked the amazed doctor.

'In a manner of speaking,' replied the beaky professor. '**My research team** at **MON-MED** created it when things got out of hand at last year's **XXXmas party.'**

The two tiny assistants looked embarrassed.

'They thought it would be funny to make a chemical that could grab hold of a monster's DNA and jiggle it about a bit. Caused all sorts of **hilarity.** Smoke pouring out of ears. Eyes revolving. But imagine our surprise the next day when we discovered that the **jiggling** also happened to cure an amazing number of monster **MALADIES!'**

'How on earth can jiggling a monster's DNA do that?' scoffed the doctor.

'Well,' said the professor, 'the actual process is far too complex to go into here. But in principle it is as simple as **untangling a headphone cable.'**

I didn't think that sounded very simple at all. In fact, I once spent an entire double maths lesson trying to **untangle** my headphone cable and somehow ended up lashed to my chair.

'We refined it and had SUCH promising results at first,' said the professor wistfully. 'Quite astonishing, really. A single dose of **FIXITALL** could completely cure previously untreatable monster conditions like **compulsive lurkivitus**⸸ or jargonese. **MON-MED** management were VERY excited . . .'

'But then you noticed the side-effects,' prompted the doctor.

'Yes,' admitted Professor Peckham, looking crestfallen. 'We found that if you try to untangle monster DNA **it often ends up even more tangled than before.** It's a bit like trying to untangle a headphone cable and ending up lashed to your chair.'

I said nothing.

'Of course, I immediately told the CEO of **MON-MED** that **FIXITALL** was **far too dangerous** to ever sell,' said the professor.

'Then why did they sell it?' I asked.

The professor sighed. 'It had something to do with all the expensive packaging that had already been printed. I forget the details . . . Ah!

Look at our patient! The **serum** is taking *effect*. How are you feeling, Philip?'

Mr Gillman's eyeballs had begun rotating in opposite directions. 'A little dizzy, Prof,' he replied. 'But no worse than being **trapped** in some of the whirlpools in the Amazon.'

'That's a little odd,' said the monster doctor. 'Surely the **nasal whining** and ear smoke come before *eyeball-rotating?*'

'Not with my serum,' explained Professor Peckham. 'It is deliberately designed to reverse the effects of **FIXITALL.** The nasal whining, ear smoke and *rotating eyeballs* all now happen in the reverse order. Which is why Mr Nimby rather amusingly calls it **ЯEVERSITALL.'** The professor's laughter was cut off by another **violent coughing** fit. Copious amounts of smoke were now pouring out from Mr Gillman's ears. Ms Tenement switched on an extractor fan.

'That's better,' the professor continued, once the **air** had cleared a little. 'Where was I?'

'You were selling dangerous **FIXITALL** to monsters,' I reminded him.

'Ah, yes, indeed,' said the professor. 'And before we knew it there were hundreds of poor monsters with **wonky walks, strange diets** and *unfashionable skin patterns* turning up at HQ and threatening to eat the CEO and senior management team. So they took fright and fled to dimension 2.6.'

Mr Gillman's nasal areas began to whine. 'So I determined to find a cure! I borrowed –' the professor looked a bit shifty – 'a few hundred gallons of **FIXITALL** and set up this lab. And by a marvellous stroke of luck, the lovely Ms Diagnosiz from sales offered to help me in any way she could.'

How clever of her. With access to a **stash** of **FIXITALL** and a *potential cure*, she could make money however the professor's experiments worked out.

The doctor pointed to where Mr Gillman's skin remained stubbornly tartan. 'It doesn't look like you've had much luck.'

'Nonsense!' sniffed the professor. 'Look.' And, as if on cue, Mr Gillman's maroon tartan pattern began to fade. It was being replaced by something else.

'Incredible!' exclaimed the doctor. 'What is that pattern? I don't recognize it.'

'Looks like **tabby cat** to me,' I said.

But Ms Tenement
was flipping quickly
through a large ring
binder of pattern

swatches. She held it up for the professor to see.

His beaky face fell.

'**Mongolian snow leopard,**' he sighed,
slumping back into his chair. 'A thirty-seven point
five per cent improvement on **maroon** tartan,
but nowhere near a cure. Blast!'

'Can't you just tweak the serum a little bit and
try again?' I asked.

'You don't understand,' he said frustratedly.
'**ЯEVERSITALL** works by using **simpler
DNA** to "smooth-out" the patient's tangled DNA.
It's a bit like taking a hopelessly tangled headphone
cable, throwing it away and just buying a nice
new one. And that batch of **ЯEVERSITALL** was
based on a **monster amoeba.** There is no
living creature anywhere with a simpler DNA

structure than that blob of gloopy slime.' He broke off, looking utterly despaired.

'Hmm . . .' the doctor said, considering for a moment. Then she turned to me and said, in a rather **smug** voice, 'Oh, there is . . . I know of one creature that only has two strands of DNA.'

'This is a poor moment for jokes, Von Sichertall!' chided the professor, and he shook his shaggy head dismissively. 'A creature with only two strands of DNA wouldn't be capable of any behaviour more **complex** than **slithering back and forth** between the TV, the fridge and the toilet. Nothing could possibly live like that.'

The doctor pushed me forward.

'Allow me to introduce my assistant,' she said. 'His name is Ozzy, and he is a human.'

HE CAN EVEN READ AND WRITE!

Chapter 12

The words were *barely* out of her mouth before my legs were **seized** by tiny (but surprisingly strong) hands. I looked down to find Ms Tenement and Mr Nimby had grabbed one each.

I couldn't move.

'Er . . . what are they doing?' I asked Professor Peckham. But he ignored me and picked up another

enormous

hypodermic syringe.
Then – rather
worryingly – he
began to
advance
towards
me.

'Don't panic,' he
tried (and failed) to reassure me. 'If
what my **illustrious former student** says is
true, then, in the name of progress, I must have a
teensy tiny sample of your blood. There is no need
to worry, though – I don't need more than sixteen –
maybe seventeen – pints. Dr Von Sichertall,' he
added, **'would you please tell your student to
stop shaking so much?** My hands aren't as
steady as they once were.'

The huge needle headed towards me, as
menacing as a **stray javelin** on sports day.

'Professor!' I protested loudly. 'As an expert on
human anatomy, I can say with some confidence
that I don't actually contain sixteen or seventeen
pints of blood.'

'Really?' said the professor. He looked disappointed. 'Well, I suppose I could use a slightly smaller needle. Would that work for you?'

I managed to breathe again. 'Nothing larger than a **monster-size extra extra extra small**, please.'

And so a few minutes later I was sticking a monster plaster on my arm and watching as Professor Peckham's machine analysed my **blood.** There was a soft CHIME and the **twisting double spiral** of human DNA appeared on one of the screens.

'*WOW!*' I said in amazement. 'So that's actually MY very own DNA.' The doctor and professor were also staring at it with a sense of complete wonder that was very flattering.

'I would never have believed it possible – if I wasn't looking at it with my own eyes,' said an awed Professor Peckham.

'I know. Incredible, isn't it?' agreed the doctor. 'I remember Professor Twinky telling us back in medical school that humans had only two strands of DNA. **I'd always assumed he was pulling everyone's tentacles.** But here –' she squeezed my arm affectionately – 'is the living proof! A creature that can walk upright, speak – albeit with an **amusing accent** – read, write and is even learning to drive a monster ambulance! The universe is clearly far stranger than any monster can imagine!'

There was another soft **CHIME** and the automated voice announced:

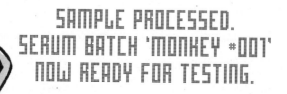

SAMPLE PROCESSED.
SERUM BATCH 'MONKEY #001'
NOW READY FOR TESTING.

The professor extracted a small vial of gloopy liquid from the machine. 'Mr Gillman,' he said. 'I realize it is an awful lot to ask of a monster, but are you prepared be tested with a serum derived from –' he paused dramatically – **'a human being?'**

The lizardy monster's head crest *twitched* with disgust. 'It's a pretty revolting thought,' Mr Gillman said. 'But, if it's a **choice** between that and wearing tartan for the rest of my life, I'm prepared to take the risk.'

'That's the spirit!' said the professor. Then, without warning, he plunged the huge needle into Mr Gillman's arm.

The swamp creature's eyes began to revolve again, and for the next few minutes the workshop was almost silent. We all waited on *tenterhooks.* The only sounds were the whirr of the extractor fan sucking Mr Gillman's ear smoke away, the **furious scratching** of Mr Nimby making observations in his tiny notebooks and – eventually – the all-too-familiar nasal whining.

Finally, Mr Gillman's skin pattern began to change from **Mongolian snow leopard** into something else. Ms Tenement stood poised by her **ring binder** full of pattern swatches. But it wasn't needed.

'**IT WORKED!**' we all cried together.

Mr Gillman's healthy, slimy scales had been restored.

The two tiny assistants embraced each other, kissed (surprisingly passionately) and began a charming little **dance of celebration.** Even Mr Gillman's head crest jiggled in the universal swamp signal for happiness.

'Oh, how marvellous!' cried the monster doctor. 'And well done, Ozzy, for being so – 'she hunted around for the right word – **'uncomplicated!'** She turned to Professor Peckham. 'How quickly can you make this slimy brilliance? Five gallons should be enough to treat all my patients.'

It only took Professor Peckham half an hour to produce a **five gallon** bottle of **ЯEVERSITALL**. While we waited, he also made a few *calls* to old friends at monster pharmaceutical companies. **ЯEVERSITALL** would soon be produced in **quantities large enough** for even a dizzy colossosaur.

We walked happily out of Unit 107 and looked around for Lance.

'**LAAAANNNNNCE!**' shouted the doctor. '**HERE, BOY! WE'RE GOING HOME!**'

'Shouldn't we call the monster police about Ms Diagnosiz?' I asked as we waited.

'**There's no point,**' replied the doctor. 'She'll be well on her way to dimension 2.6 by now. Sitting on *lovely* red-hot swamp sand, drinking freshly squeezed bile juice and counting her ill-gotten gains – now where is that silly ambulance? Probably rooting through the bins for spare parts, if I know him. **LAAAAANNNNCE!**' she screeched.

There was a loud revving, followed by the sounds of banging and clanging coming from behind a **row of garages**.

'I knew it!' cried the doctor as we ran towards the noise. 'What are you up to back there, you naughty ambulance?'

We rounded the corner into the alleyway and came face to face with Lance's rear end. His *wheels* were *spinning* like a **bull pawing the ground** and he kept lunging at something trapped further down the alleyway.

'Oh, what have you got hold of now?' groaned the doctor. 'I swear, one day you'll try on some garish bumper that *doesn't even suit you* and catch a horrid disease like **fender rot.** And then where will you be? DROP IT! I said, DROP IT!'

The excited ambulance obeyed the doctor and reversed out of the alley to reveal the shiny black car of Ms Diagnosiz.

And there, with her tiny hands on the **steering wheel**, was the glum-looking saleswoman herself.

'GOOD BOY!' praised the doctor as she patted Lance. 'Who's a clever boy? You are! Yes, you are!' She tickled his *wing mirror* and the ambulance revved happily.

Ms Diagnosiz wound down the limo's window and *hitched* on her toothy smile. 'Hello, Dr Sichertall,' she said as innocently as someone with two hundred and forty-seven huge teeth can. 'I can explain everything—'

'No, you can't,' interrupted the doctor. 'Your greedy, irresponsible behaviour might have **harmed** my patients! And imagine if poor, delicate, defenceless Mr Gorgonzilla had injured himself when he fell over! *What a loss to monster ballet* that would have been.'

I could see Ms Diagnosiz thought the idea of a five-thousand-tonne colossosaur being injured by *falling over* was as **ridiculous** as I did. But she knew to stay quiet in the face of such a serious monster ballet fan.

'Luckily for you,' continued the doctor in a calmer tone, 'my **primitive** assistant, Ozzy, has once again saved the day. So perhaps we should **all** treat this as a **"teaching moment"**. Me to put all thoughts of a "universal cure" to one side, and you to go and find yourself a more **ethical career.** Use your **undoubtable sales talents** on something nice and safe, like **volcano time-share villas.'**

The saleswoman nodded gratefully. 'I am very sorry for the mix-up, Doctor. Maybe you're right. My sisters have always wanted me to join the family custom-denture business, Pointy Sisters Prosthetics.'

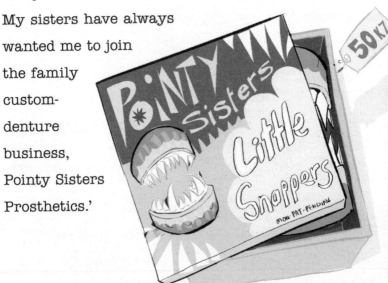

'A fine company,' said the doctor sharply. 'I'm wearing a set from their "Little Snappers" range right now.'

'Perhaps I'll give that a go,' said Ms Diagnosiz. **'I'm dreadfully sorry for all the trouble I've caused.'**

'LANCE! RELEASE HER!' called the doctor, and the ambulance backed away reluctantly. Ms Diagnosiz seized the opportunity and drove away quickly for a career in orthodontics – although not quickly enough to prevent Lance from 'accidentally on purpose' clipping the IDV's one *remaining* wing mirror clean off.

A LOVELY SINGALONG

Chapter 13

So the doctor and I went home.

The journey took a bit *longer* than expected as we got stuck for a while in dimension 3.9.

We were just pulling up in front of the surgery when Delores came *skipping gaily* towards us. Sadly there was still a **HUGE** smile on her face.

'Doctor!' she cried happily. 'How simply marvellous to see you – and the lovely Ozzy – back home so soon. As you can see, everything is going *wonderfully* well here.'

'Excellent. So the patients are all still in the waiting room, then?' the doctor asked.

'Not as such,' said Delores.

'But I specifically told you to keep them in here,' the doctor cried.

'I know,' admitted the horrifically apologetic receptionist. 'But, you see, I ran out of tea and biscuits about an hour ago and there were *ever such a lot* of **grumpy faces**. Still, you know me, Doctor – always trying to cheer everyone up. So I **slithered up** on my desk and started a lovely *community singalong* of old show tunes. You remember **'All the Fun of the Graveyard!'**, **'My Old Man's a Dust-Monster'** and, my favourite, *'I Left My Heart in Your Bedside Cabinet.'*

She began to hum a creepy yet somehow surprisingly **catchy** pop song. 'And before too long I had everyone up on their feet and **jumping** around so much they simply had to get outside! And they were enjoying themselves SO MUCH I couldn't get them to come back in.'

As she was talking, I noticed that Oswalt Sadbottom was trying to **conceal himself** in the doorway of Mrs Scabies's Ye Olde Flea Shop.

But he had to keep hopping from one leg to the other to avoid falling over. And there was Simon Salamander, desperately attempting to blend into a **JOIN THE MONSTER MARINES CORPSE** poster on

the **opposite side** of the road – but was given away by the violently coloured stripes on his skin.

In fact, a closer look revealed the rest of the doctor's patients all *desperately attempting* to hide from Delores's enforced community fun.

I pointed this out to the doctor while Delores continued humming loudly to herself.

'Blast!' the doctor whispered. 'We'll never get the patients back to the surgery with Delores in this **terrifyingly** *cheerful mood.* And they urgently need the **ЯEVERSITALL!'**

I looked around at the terrified monsters. 'I think I've got an idea . . .' I said. 'Pass me the **ЯEVERSITALL** bottle, please. And, Lance, be a good chap and run your *extendable ladder* up to the third floor.' In seconds I was out through Lance's sunroof, *scampering up* his **ladder** and hopping through the window of the swamp-spa treatment room.

'**GOOOD AFTERNOOOON, OZEEEE!**' said Spurtie as he spotted me. '**DOOO YOOO WANNN ANOTHHERRR WOSHHHH?**'

'Yes please, Spurtie,' I said eagerly. 'But can you use this *extra-special shampoo*, please?' I unpacked the barrel of **FIXITALL** antidote and unscrewed the cap.

'**OOOOH!**' said the shower snake as he stuck his tail into it. '**TASTES LOOOVLY!**' Then he began to greedily suck up the slimy substance.

I grabbed his nozzle head, pointed it out of the window and shouted, '*HEY, EVERYONE! I'VE FOUND DELORES'S HIDDEN BISCUIT STASH!*'

Immediately, there was a **tremendous rumbling** as all the monsters in the **street** below (including Delores) left their hiding places and *rushed* towards the surgery's entrance.

'HIT IT, SPURTIE!' I yelled, and the shower snake began to rain **ЯEVERSITALL** all over Lovecraft Avenue.

The barrel was barely empty before the eyeballs of every monster in the street started **spinning** in opposite directions. When the ear-smoking phase began, Lovecraft Avenue became **completely engulfed in smoke.** The only things still visible were the tops of **lamp posts** and Oswalt Sadbottom's damp comb-over.

By the time I got down the stairs and back outside, the **smoke** was clearing and even the massed nasal whining was coming to an end.

Simon Salamander was back to his usual healthy pinky-green. Vlad and Vladness were spitting out the remains of **celery from their teeth.** Even Oswalt Sadbottom's legs seemed to be approximately the same length again. From what I could tell, everyone was completely healed of their nasty **FIXITALL** side-effects!

Even Delores.

Her face was back to being as **dark** and **threatening** as the **inside of a troll's ear canal.** She brandished her empty biscuit tin in one tentacle and a large collection of **unwashed mugs** in the other seven. 'All my special biscuits gone! All this washing-up to do! Blooming patients! The doctor should snip off their limbs and **superglue** them back on in completely the wrong places. She should peel off their tentacled tips and dip them in **salt-and-vinegar crisps.** She should . . . Why are you smiling?' she snapped at me.

I patted her on the nearest tentacle. 'Because it's so nice to have you back to normal, Delores,'

I said, and she was so confused that she *slithered* away without saying anything rude.

The doctor and I watched as the last of the **patients** wandered off, heading back to their houses, caves, graves and **coffins.**

'Well done, Ozzy!' said the doctor. 'And no doubt they'll all be back tomorrow with their in-growing **eyeballs,** scarlet weasel-measles and broken tongues that need urgent splinting . . .'

She broke off and smiled at me. 'I should have listened to you, Ozzy. There'll never be a cure for all illness. The answer for monster maladies is medicine – not magic!'

We stepped back into the surgery. 'Still, we mustn't grumble.' She laughed. 'I actually got to meet Gorgonzilla! **Now run along and fetch me** a number twenty-seven needle and thread.'

'What for?' I asked.

'Have you forgotten Morty, Nurse Ozzy?' she chided. 'He's still in a collection of *carrier bags* in reception. I'll go and ask him where his missing right leg is, and then together we'll **STITCH** up your **clumsy zombie friend.**'

THE END

GORGONZILLA

PRIVATE BOX FOR TWO MONSTERS (OR ORDINARIES)

KAIJU PRODUCTIONS

INVITES YOU TO THE PREMIERE
OF AN EARTH-SHATTERING NEW WORK

BY AWARD-WINNING COLOSSO-CHOREOGRAPHER

RODANO!

STARRING

GORGONZILLA & MILLICENT MOTH

[Date & Venue To Be Confirmed]

GLOSSARY

Acne: A healthy layer of angry sores covering up the unpleasant face of a young human. One of the few times that monsters don't find humans completely disgusting to look at.

Bell-bug: Small monsters who communicate with each other by clanging their hard metal shells. Bell-bug species come in different musical keys and can therefore be played together as a charming musical instrument. Sadly, as F# & Bb bell-bugs are now extinct, the bell-bug musical repertoire has become somewhat limited.

Celebrity: A term used to describe a human being who is well known for having the amazing ability to be well known.

166

Compulsive lurkivitus: An affliction that causes monsters to feel an overwhelming desire to conceal themselves in ridiculous spaces and snigger quietly at their friends or family. If your relative is missing, try the loft, the space beneath the bed or the back of the wardrobe behind the outdoor coats. Failing that, just open a large box of chocolates noisily, and wait.

Executive: A highly prized job in the human world. The job title denotes that an employee is so good at their job that they no longer have to do it.

Fender rot (also known as bumper rot): An unpleasant mould that spoils the shiny parts of inter-dimensional vehicles. It can be caught by frequenting unsanitary garages or through the revolting practice of swapping hubcaps with strangers.

Flatulence: One of the most moving musical art forms ever devised.

Grandpa: An elderly human male. Easily identifiable as they have removed most of their head hair and inserted it forcibly into their ear and nasal cavities. No one knows why they do this.

Homework: A particularly cruel and unusual human torture technique involving large amounts of paper and small sharpened sticks.

'I Left My Heart in Your Bedside Cabinet': A slow and tender ballad from the legendary monster singer Awreatha Fangling. She was better known for her more up-tempo hits such as 'Stalking After Midnight' and 'Radio Gaaargh-Gaaargh'.

Manicure: A human process that is quite similar to the monster practice of claw-sharpening. One major difference is that in the human version manicurists are very rarely eaten by their dissatisfied customers.

Mega-Jenga: The rules are the same as the popular human party game Jenga. But a monster Mega-Jenga block is 50 feet long, made of concrete and weighs over 200 tonnes. The game requires any of the following: teamwork, very large muscles or access to heavy construction machinery.

Modern monster ballet: Traditional monster ballet has easily understandable plots full of romance, tragedy and the thrill of stamping large buildings flat. Modern monster ballet, however, claims these are 'cliches' and favours the dancers looking serious while standing on one leg or tentacle and wearing a brightly coloured, ill-fitting leotard. It is not very popular.

Mr Woffell: An unusually talented teacher at Ozzy's School. Mr Woffell has the incredible ability of being able to talk about any subject, for any length of time, without either breathing or communicating any useful information at all.

Patient riot: These are usually caused by long waiting times, extremely rude receptionists and desperate hunger caused by broken vending machines. Fortunately, most patient riots end quite quickly. Especially since sleeping-gas sprinklers became a common feature of doctors' surgeries.

Salad: Vegetables that you can eat. As opposed to vegetables that can eat you. See: Triffids, Razor Radishes and Spring-loaded Onions.

Tartan: Centuries ago, the Scottish people decided that it was far too confusing to have to choose between fabric with a spotted, striped or diagonal pattern. So they replaced all three patterns with a single new one: the Tartan!

Unfortunately, people immediately began to modify the original design. As a consequence, there are now approximately 18,694,290 different tartans.

Daily Fang: The most popular vampire newspaper. It has a winning combination of sharp incisive journalism, biting commentary and an excellent recipe section. A much easier read than its worthy (but rather dull) rival *The Whole Tooth*.

XXXmas party: Once a year, sensible monsters gather together beneath damp bridges, in dark cellars or in their charming Swedish-style open-plan chalets to celebrate *XXX*mas. They drink, eat their least popular relatives and pass the time playing traditional games like Pasta-parcel, Blind Monster's Huff and Table Pong-pong.

Turn the page to read an exclusive extract from
Ozzy and the doctor's next hilarious adventure

the
MONSTER
DOCTOR
Foul Play

It will have you laughing your head off!

GHASTLY COLOUR COMBINATION

Chapter 1

I had just turned the corner into Lovecraft Avenue when a head-sized object came *flying* through the air towards me. Without thinking, I caught it. Then I peered down and realised that it wasn't just 'head-sized'.

It actually was a head.

A **scruffy, smelly** and **smiley head** with a friendly face that I recognised at once.

'Hello Morty!' I said.

'Where's the rest of you today?'

My friend Morty is a **Level-1 registered dead person** (or a zombie to you) and therefore his arms, legs, eyeballs and belly buttons are only attached to each other with **MY DODGY STITCHING,** or lashings, of ICBINS super-glue.

'Oh! Hello Ozzy!' Morty replied, grinning up at me with his **gap-toothed mouth**. 'Never mind that now. What a lovely catch! **Bravo!** I didn't know you were playing.'

'Playing what?' I asked, confused.

I should note here that one of the reasons Morty's body parts are often in several places at once is because he's always felt that being dead shouldn't get in the way of his sporting hobbies. He plays *mugball* (Monster rugby), **zombie football, mixed monster martial arts**

(MMMA) and – on one memorable but catastrophic occasion – he even went **bungee-jumping.**

'Why, we're playing **Monsterball** of course!' Morty laughed. 'Surely you know that today is the Dimension 3 Monsterball Championship finals?'

I looked at him blankly. As I always do whenever anyone mentions human sports like Kickball, Basket-hoop or Runny-Jump-thing. I forget their names. So, I'm sorry if I've given you the impression that I'm not a big fan of sports.

It shouldn't be an impression.

I'm as fond of human sports as I am of **scraping the cheese out from between a troll's toes.** So monster sports couldn't be any better.

'Never mind,' continued Morty, 'a few of us thought we'd celebrate *cup final day* by having a nice friendly amateur game here in Lovecraft Avenue.'

'Who is 'we'?' I asked. But the words were barely out of my mouth before there was **a loud roar** and **a mob of hideously ugly monsters** charged out of the alleyway that runs down the side of that new ghoul fashion boutique, **'DIG-IT!'**

I wasn't frightened. You see being **'hideously ugly'** is completely normal for monsters. And after spending the summer working for the monster doctor, the sight of **slobbering jaws, razor-sharp horns** and **quivering eye-stalks** isn't any more frightening than my Granny Freda's *sherry & lavender flavoured moustache.*

The mob all sported scarves with the same ghastly colour combination: *Rabid Red and Yahoo Yellow stripes.* I recognised regular patients like **Bob the Blob,** who was slithering rapidly along in a thick slick of his own **snot.** There was Mr Gillman, a swamp creature who'd recently moved into one of the new super-damp basement flats beneath the **snake-grooming parlour.** And at the head of the mob was the **fifteen stone of thrashing tentacles, temper and tasteless knitwear** that was Delores, the charmless receptionist from the monster doctor's surgery.

Before we go any further, I should probably let you know that Delores once scored **12.3** on the **inter-dimensional standardised monster grumpiness test.** Which is pretty amazing since the test only goes up to 10.

So you can imagine exactly how I felt when she pointed a **quivering tentacle** in my direction

and bellowed – in a voice like a T. Rex auditioning for the role of an evil pirate captain in a pantomime –
'AWFUL ALL-STARS! ATTACK!'

The mob of monsters following her roared in response and charged straight at me.

'Morty,' I said, as calmly as I could manage in the circumstances, 'why are Delores and those patients charging at me?'

Morty grinned. 'They're not charging at you, Ozzy.' And before I could check whether his eyes had fallen out again (they often do) he added, **'They're charging at ME!'**

'Ah!' I said. As if that made the slightest difference. I was, after all, currently holding him. 'Is there any particular reason why?' I was hoping that he'd come up with an answer that didn't include us both ending up as **flat as Lucy Liverwort** when she got caught in the *triple-chocolate-toffee cake* **stampede** in the school canteen last year. Tragic.

'Like I said,' my zombie friend replied, 'we decided to play **Monsterball.** But as the ball said she was feeling a bit sick – someone she ate, apparently – I volunteered to take her place!'

As answers go that clearly wasn't a great deal of help.

Luckily, the monster doctor had taught me to always keep an eye out for a *potential escape route* – a vital skill for any trainee monster doctor. You never know when you'll need a quick getaway from an **angry** or **dissatisfied** patient! So as the **fangs, horns, teeth** and **slobber** of the AWFUL ALL-STARS bore down on me I tucked Morty under my arm and began edging towards an alleyway to my right.

Unfortunately, just as I was about to make a break for it, a second (and equally hideously ugly) **mob of monsters** erupted from that alleyway too.

Oh, super.

This new lot were headed by Vlad, the vampire who runs the all-night convenience store on the corner of Lovecraft Lane and Cushing St. It was made up of his regulars like Colin the Ghoul, Simon Salamander from the **Battered Squid Chippie** and Mrs Stunck, a very nice jellified thing who lives in one of the larger bins round the back of the restaurant.

With the depressing inevitability of a **bad mark in a maths test**, the second mob spotted Morty and howled, '**FANGTON FANTOMS NEVER DIE!**' Then they put their heads down (or whatever passed for a head) and charged straight for us.

Two monster mobs. Me in the middle.

I groaned with disappointment.

It wasn't the **imminent danger**, as such. After all, a typical day as an assistant monster doctor isn't complete without **extreme danger**. For instance, so far this month I'd been **eaten, blown-up, covered in foul-smelling bodily fluids** (most days) and last Wednesday was even carried aloft to an impressive height of 17,000ft in the claws of a **SHORT-SIGHTED DRAGON MOTHER** who mistook me for her **BABY DRAGLING**.

No. I was disappointed because I hadn't even had a chance to sit down and prepare myself for the day with a nice cup of Coughee and a chocolate indigestive!

It was so unfair!

And that was when I was suddenly distracted by a wastepaper bin shouting at me.

TO BE CONTINUED . . .

ACKNOWLEDGEMENTS

Huge thanks are owed to the following people who helped bring you these silly pages.

My wife, Cathy, whose never-ending weirdness and unacknowledged acting genius is the inspiration for 48.3% of the monster characters. (I'm not telling you who the other 51.7% are based on.)

Jodie, Emily, Molly and everyone at United Agents for opening up a whole new dimension for the monster doctor and Ozzy to explore.

And, finally, Cate, Amanda, Sue, Rachel and all the amazingly hard-working and talented people at Macmillan. I couldn't have completed this book without their calm and creative support – especially in that final exhausted push to the finish line.

ABOUT THE AUTHOR

John Kelly is the author and illustrator of picture books such as *The Beastly Pirates* and *Fixer*, the author of picture books *Can I Join Your Club* and *Hibernation Hotel*, and the illustrator of fiction series such as Ivy Pocket and Araminta Spook. He has twice been shortlisted for the Kate Greenaway prize, with *Scoop!* and *Guess Who's Coming for Dinner*. The Monster Doctor is his first author-illustrator middle-grade fiction series.